POTENTIAL WEAPONS

POTENTIAL WEAPONS

༺∽༻

A Novella and Stories

Jocelyn Lieu

Graywolf Press
Saint Paul, Minnesota

Publication of this volume is made possible in part by a grant provided by the Minnesota State Arts Board, through an appropriation
by the Minnesota State Legislature; a grant from the Wells Fargo
Foundation Minnesota; and a grant from the National Endowment
for the Arts. Significant support has also been provided by the
Bush Foundation; Target, Marshall Field's and Mervyn's with support from the Target Foundation; the McKnight Foundation; and
other generous contributions from foundations, corporations, and
individuals. To these organizations and individuals we offer our
heartfelt thanks.

MINNESOTA
STATE ARTS BOARD

NATIONAL
ENDOWMENT
FOR THE ARTS

Published by Graywolf Press
2402 University Avenue, Suite 203
Saint Paul, Minnesota 55114
All rights reserved.

www.graywolfpress.org

Published in the United States of America
Printed in Canada

ISBN 1-55597-397-3

2 4 6 8 9 7 5 3 1
First Graywolf Printing, 2004

Library of Congress Control Number: 2003111081

Cover design: Kyle G. Hunter

Cover photograph: © Corbis. All Rights Reserved.

For Chuck and Gracie

Acknowledgments

I am grateful for all of their help to Kathleen Anderson, Dore Ashton and Matti Megged, Charles Baxter, Donna Brody, William Clark, Anne Czarniecki, Katie Dublinski, Parker Huang, Ben Huang, Noble and Carolyn Lieu, Margot Livesey, Michael Martone, Steven Schwartz, Jim Shepard, Joan Silber, Robert Simpson, John Skoyles, and especially Chuck Wachtel. In addition, I would like to thank the Millay Colony for the Arts, Ucross Foundation, and the Writers Room.

"The Children" first appeared in the *Asian Pacific American Journal*, "Safety" in the *Denver Quarterly*, and "This World" in *Charlie Chan Is Dead: An Anthology of Contemporary Asian American Fiction*.

Contents

POTENTIAL WEAPONS

∽

Holding the road map at arm's length, Abi Leong's mother, Alice, frowned over the edge of her glasses as though the crisscrossed lines contained a hidden message that would be revealed if only she could stare them down. Without the thick lenses, her blue eyes looked unnaturally small. Alice was so nearsighted as to be legally blind. Over the years she'd grown farsighted as well, yet she refused to give in to bifocals. "It's not vanity," she'd told Abi. "It's another form of resistance. One day you'll understand."

Abi gazed out the windshield at the empty road and gray sky. Winter had given way to a cool, rainy spring. Some of the fields were newly plowed, and the disturbed earth gleamed black and wet. This was the kind of country—flat, fertile, serious—where you could actually feel the gravity hold you to the ground. Although it had been eight months since she'd moved to Indiana, Abi still wasn't sure why she was there. At the moment, in her Subaru with her mother, who was visiting from New York—the city Abi never should have left—being there had the claustrophobic feel of fate.

They were driving to a Ku Klux Klan rally in a town called Clarion. Going hadn't been Abi's idea. For her, protest was a thorny business with no real right or wrong.

1

Besides, she was afraid—not of the Klan, exactly, but of the possibility of violence and other possibilities she hadn't yet named. Not that her fears mattered. At breakfast on the second day of her visit, her mother had read about the upcoming rally in the *Tippecanoe Courier*. Rattling the newspaper in Abi's direction, she'd said, "Look at him, will you? A Grand Dragon for the new millennium." Abi peered at the photo of a plump-cheeked white man in a gray jacket, black slacks, and striped ochre tie. The man—who, like her, was in his early thirties—stood on the county courthouse steps, clutching an ungainly brief-case. Grand Dragon. He could just as well have been a junior-level executive in a company that manufactured wall anchors or venetian blinds.

"Let's go, hon. Don't you want to look evil in the face?" Alice's eyes, for the first time since Abi's father had died, had shone openly with joy.

"I think I've solved the mystery," she said now. "Stay on this road. Keep heading south. It's simple. Once you figure it out, everything in this state of yours is simple."

Abi knew that the moment you left the highways, north-central Indiana dissolved into a frustrating web of back roads. Maps were useless. Roads could unexpectedly circle or dead-end at bridges that had been washed out for years.

"My state? Who says it's mine?"

"Well, one of us lives here, and it sure isn't me."

Grinning, Alice refolded the map. She was no stranger to what she called the Dark Heartland of America. Before moving to New York at the age of eighteen, she had grown up on a farm near Hutchinson, Kansas. There was a whole side of the family Abi knew only from photographs: light-haired, smiling strangers who began in sepia and ended in the faded colors of the first Kodak snapshots. The summer she was five, Abi actually visited Kansas with her mother. In Kansas, the clouds were large and silent. One afternoon, a hawk flew into the picture window. Her grandfather wrapped the stunned bird in a towel and laid it on the kitchen table. Abi's grandmother said, "She'll remember this moment for the rest of her life," and so far she did, but she barely remembered her grandparents. Soon they became photographs again, and after they'd died—within a year of each other—and the farm was sold and debts paid, Abi had received a check for two hundred twenty-six dollars, their legacy.

"Mom," she said, "maybe it's better to stay away. There's that other rally across town. I think they're calling it a unity celebration."

Alice withdrew two rubber balls from her bag. Squeezing them helped fend off the rheumatoid arthritis that assailed her hands. Although they'd been reunited for only three days, the habit was already wearing on Abi's nerves.

"Unity," her mother murmured.

The balls were Spaldings, the same kind Abi had played handball with when she was a kid.

"Unity *celebration*. Sounds dull as dishwater." Alice's fists closed over the hard pink globes. "What does one *do* at a unity celebration? Unify?"

Abi directed her gaze back out at the gray and black world. A ray of fast-fading light fell on three squat white silos, making them glow like obese angels. Here was a life her mother might have lived if she'd stayed where she'd been born, a life of houses with pitched roofs and a single tree in each yard—a stick-figure dream of a world that Abi had drawn over and over when she was a child, despite the fact that the Leongs had lived in an apartment on the Upper West Side. In her pictures, the skin of the mother, father, and child was always the crayon color they used to call Flesh.

"Eyes on the road, honey," Alice said. "Tired? Want me to take over? It's been awhile, but I think I can still pilot one of these things."

"Mom, I'm fine."

They passed a few moments without speaking.

"You sure we want to do this?" Abi said at last. "I mean, what if it gets ugly?"

Her mother's stiff fingers squeezed. "People can get ugly. That's certainly true."

Suddenly, Alice turned and stared at Abi as if she'd remembered something she was horrified to have forgotten.

"You're *afraid*, hon."

Abi smiled. "I'm not. No more than I should be, anyway."

"Of course you are. This is your first real demonstration. You're like a soldier going into battle for the first time, not only afraid of injury and death and enemies and all, but of your own reaction." She nodded knowingly. "This will be nothing, I promise. And even if it *does* turn into something, we'll live through it."

The horizon ahead was broken by a low line of trees, which meant they were approaching Clarion. A dark blot hovered in the sky. At first Abi thought it was a hawk and, grateful for the chance to change the subject, was on the verge of pointing it out until she realized it was a helicopter.

The police helicopter slowly circled. Was her mother right in naming her fear? Was she, in effect, afraid of herself? Before the thought could take hold, she pushed it to the edge of her consciousness, where she had deposited so many of her mother's other ideas.

When they came to the sign that said they were entering Clarion, Population 4,508, Alice tucked the handballs back into her purse.

"I'm not interested in your unity celebration," she said. "In my time, I've heard enough talk about what's good and right. I know it's hard, hon, but make your old ma happy. Take her to where the action is."

Although three years had passed since her father's death, Abi still wasn't used to being alone with her mother. What she missed most about her father was the laughter. Her parents had known how to laugh. While Abi's cheeks burned with shame, they'd laughed at the Chinese cooks who'd come out of the kitchen to stare at the Chinese man, the white woman, and their mixed-up daughter. They laughed at the barely concealed astonishment that— in the early years, at least—met them at every turn. They laughed off the fact that his family persisted in calling Alice "Luther's German wife," although she didn't possess a single drop of German blood. They even laughed when her family refused to call Luther anything at all.

Sometimes, when they argued about fine points in literature or history, Abi's father would say, "Your ancestors were living in caves and painting themselves blue while mine were composing poetry." Although it was an old joke, told year after year, they'd both howl.

When she was a teenager, Abi got angry at her parents for laughing so much. "Stop *denying*," she'd tell them. "You deny the gravest things." And they would stop, for a moment, but Abi knew it was only because they didn't want to hurt her feelings.

Laughter was what joined them together; it was their weapon. But then, on a Wednesday in April, Abi's father collapsed at the podium in a lecture hall filled with his students. He fell into a coma, from which he never emerged, dying two hours after Alice and Abi arrived at the hospital. Alice said she was grateful for those hours, for that one small mercy. While Abi stood helplessly beside the bed, her mother leaned down and held him. Alice gazed into her husband's face, her own face suffused with a strange beauty. Abi stared at her father, too, studying him, trying to memorize every feature. Hating herself for not having looked more fully while he was alive.

In the weeks and months that followed, Abi rarely cried out loud. Grief was confusing. The thought that she was half an orphan haunted her. The selfishness of loss made her prickle with guilt. Her mother, though, grieved fully and well. She cried when she talked about her memories and when they went together to places that reminded her of him. In restaurants, Abi waited half enviously while her mother removed her glasses and publicly wept. After a minute or two, she would smile, daub her eyes, and announce that she was going to the bathroom to repair herself.

"Go ahead, hon, don't stand on ceremony. Eat up," she'd say.

After a year or so of this, Abi decided to go to graduate school. Since her father's death, she'd grown impatient with meaningless things. Her job, in the publicity department of a publishing house, brought her no closer to the books she loved. The idea of change slightly unnerved her, however. When Abi confessed to feeling uncomfortable about possibly leaving New York and leaving her alone, Alice scolded her. "Don't be ridiculous. Get on with that life of yours. Isn't it about time?"

Secretly, Abi applied only to schools in the Midwest,

her mother's country. Of all corners of America, it seemed the most calm, bland, and sane. When she imagined the Midwest, she imagined clapboard houses, neatly mowed lawns, wisteria, porch swings, cloud-dotted skies, and smiling neighbors who said things like "Hello there" and "Some weather we're having." The Midwest was a place where she could quietly slip from one life into the next.

So clear was her picture of the Midwest that at first she almost didn't notice the Confederate-flag bumper stickers and jackets, or the flags themselves hung behind dusty second-story windows. When someone chalked swastikas on the sidewalk outside the English department, she felt a rush of dismay, which faded soon enough. When several of the freshman composition students she taught as a TA wrote papers arguing against abortion, gay rights, immigration, and affirmative action—which they said was unfair to *real* Americans—she tried to see the opportunity to teach them something about tolerance and sound reasoning. When a Black student was badly beaten at a frat party—supposedly for dancing with a white woman—she was stunned. An unfortunate but isolated incident, the university president said. She disagreed and didn't, a confusion similar to grief, but quieter. Most of the people around her seemed decent, the way she understood Midwesterners were supposed to be. If they sometimes smiled too hard, as though smiling might bridge the unbridgeable distance between them, it was easy enough to forgive.

Then one day at the Tippecanoe Mall, where she'd gone to buy curtain rods, twin boys no older than seven or eight years old yelled at her in singsong and pulled their eyes into slits. "Are you their mother?" she asked the woman in the pink sweat suit walking behind them.

Casting her a look of unmistakable hatred, the woman nodded. Abi's face burned. Too shocked to react, reprimand, or teach, she ducked into the next department store to walk among the lingerie and perfumes until the ringing in her ears stopped.

After that, she couldn't ignore what she already knew. Signs were everywhere, in the casual smiles she gave that were returned by blank or hostile stares, in the personal ads filled with white Christian males seeking white Christian females, love bowling, fishing, kids OK.

Just the other day, there was a letter to the editor by a man from Independence, urging all good citizens to attend the Klan rally.

> There is one belief we should support, that being to preserve the white race. We are in danger of becoming extinct. It seems white women don't care about the white race any more. There is a conspiracy. Do you read in the history books stating where there was once an all white race but now it no longer exists? Think on it. Does this make me a racist? I think not.

Redneck. Ignorant fool. Abi's rage seemed to well up out of nowhere, like the strength people are said to summon in times of danger that enables them to lift cars off the wounded, or, wounded themselves, walk miles through the frozen night in search of rescue. The power of her anger frightened her. It was as if it had been growing silently for years and had only been waiting for someone to give it a name.

A week later, Abi read the letter aloud to her mother, hoping she would share her concealed fury and, as always, flash just the right rapier phrase. Instead, Alice laughed so hard she had to lift her glasses and wipe her eyes. She'd laughed the same way when, on the drive from the airport, they'd passed the billboard standing in a plowed field that said, US OUT OF THE UN.

"'Does this make me a racist? I think not.' I think not. What a hoot! Read it again, hon."

Then she fell quiet, and Abi knew she was remembering her husband and how he, too, would have appreciated the joke.

Clarion was a town like any of the dozen or so Indiana towns Abi had seen when she'd driven all over the state in search of her imagined Midwest. The main street was lined with carpenter Victorians. Faded American flags hung from flagpole after flagpole. Clustered on Clarion's lawns were deer, dwarves, dressed-up geese. A child's bicycle lying across a sidewalk, crosshatched with shadows cast by a leafless tree, was the only sign of life.

Gradually the houses gave way to brick and quarrystone storefronts. Police sawhorses blocked the side streets. One or two officers stood at each corner, guarding the gates of the ghost city.

By Alice's reckoning they were no more than a few blocks from the county courthouse, where the Klan would be. Abi pulled the Subaru to a stop in front of a drugstore. In the store's darkened window were a wheelchair with the footrests folded up and, next to it, a pyramid made of stacked rolls of Bounty paper towels.

A policeman wearing mirrored sunglasses walked slowly past. Trying not to look at him, Abi got out, slammed her door, and went to the passenger side. Shooing away Abi's helping hand, her mother lifted one leg then the other out onto the curb. Slowly, using the door for support, she pulled herself to standing. From her voluminous black shoulder bag, she extracted her collapsible cane.

The policeman was watching them carefully now. His sunglasses reflected Abi and Alice in curved miniature. For an instant, she saw what he must see: two women dressed in gray and black, shades not favored by the people of this place. They were citified, suspect, but women all the same—women with the same rounded back, the same stubborn jut to the chin. The old one was white, the other one foreign, Oriental. Without a doubt, though, they were mother and daughter. Which could only mean one thing.

The skin over her throat tingled with anxiety, a sensation like television snow. "Mom"—she spoke loudly, so the cop could hear—"you got any quarters? Dimes? I seem to see a meter here."

She dug around in the pouch slung around her waist, found a few pennies, a nickel, a paper clip. Not enough.

"Mom," she said again. "Change. I need some change."

Although it must have been a burden to her, Alice's bag was always full. When Abi was a child, she'd thought the unending supply of subway tokens, pens, tissues, rubber bands, keys to forgotten doors, broken necklaces, cough drops, flashlights, and the like was nothing less than magical. In later years, Alice increased her load by cylinders of cayenne mace, a Swiss Army knife, jars and bottles of homeopathic and prescription drugs, tiger balm, and, as she said, "every analgesic known to womankind."

The Velcro clasps made a tearing sound. "Just how much do you need, hon?"

Abi peered at the meter, but it was too late, her mother

had already turned to face the policeman. "Officer. Yes, you."

"Ma'am?"

Alice held a few coins in the scooped-out hollow of her palm. "How much tribute do you require? For your meter, I mean."

The policeman broke into a smile. He was, Abi saw, no older than twenty-two or -three. "That's not necessary today, ma'am."

"Oh? Why not? Is it a holiday?"

"You could call it that. Though not for us. *Definitely* not for us."

He spoke with a drawl. One front tooth overlapped the other, but he didn't seem self-conscious about it. While Abi waited, her mother interrogated him about the rally. He told Alice it wasn't far, just three and a half blocks away. She'd hear the loudspeakers; all she had to do was follow the sound. There was a checkpoint, he said. A checkpoint? Yes, a checkpoint where they'd have to stop and be searched, and surrender any potential weapons.

"Well, I thank you," Alice said. "You've been very helpful. Keep the peace."

"We try our best, ma'am."

The officer moved one blue sawhorse aside so Abi and her mother could pass. "You take care of yourself now, ma'am."

"I always do."

Together, the two women walked slowly down the street. The cane made a rubbery thump on the concrete.

"My, what an innocent!" Alice said.

"Hush, Mom, he'll hear." Abi couldn't help smiling. They passed a women's clothing store. The undressed mannequins in the window, which had painted hair and blue-eye-shadowed eyes, were wrapped in white paper to cover their nakedness.

"Such a nice boy," Alice said, almost sadly. "Hear the country in his voice? Good country people. Who would've known they still exist?"

The booming sound growing louder and louder was, Abi realized, recorded country-western music. A slide guitar echoed hollowly off the limestone walls, mixing with the low, throaty beat of the helicopter.

When they turned the corner, it was as if they'd stepped into another world. A sea of people filled the street, slowly moving across the intersection ahead. Brightly dressed, like a crowd going to a county fair, they transformed the space between buildings into a roil of cinematic color and light. The rally was real after all, and she and her mother were almost there.

Alice was right, she'd never been to a demonstration where people gathered in public to shout their passions for and against, where anger was hurled into the open, all skin torn off polite talk, the equation turned to Us or Them. Or rather she had, but as an infant pushed in a stroller by her mother, who had marched to protest American involvement in the Vietnam War.

To say she was afraid of *herself*, however, seemed an absurd idea, when there was so much more to be afraid of.

"Mom, we can still leave," she said. "It's not too late."

"It's never too late." Abi's mother didn't stop walking. "Hon, I can't speak for you, but I have to go. Silence is consent, and all."

They were close enough now so that Abi could see individual people. A very fat woman wearing a sweatshirt

with a head-sized bumblebee appliquéd on the front
ambled past. Near her was a thin boy in denim who had
a Confederate flag wrapped bandit-style around his face.
Abi and her mother stepped into the crowd. Somehow she
found herself next to the bandit boy, whose long adolescent
legs moved with the angular strides of a sandhill crane.

Above them all rose the pale dome of the Clarion
County courthouse. The banner strung across its façade
read, MARCH IS DISABILITY AWARENESS MONTH.
On a roof across the street, an American flag snapped
in the damp wind. A police sniper kneeled in silhouette
below, his rifle braced against his ribs. The helicopter
hovered over him, then veered away.

On the street were more sawhorses and, behind them,
a long line of cops in helmets who held curved Plexiglas
shields. The shieldless police at either end of the line
cradled nightsticks or rifles with bores so wide Abi imagined that she could see the tear-gas canisters nestled in
their chambers.

"Quite a show. I think we're supposed to be impressed,"
Alice said.

"It's still not too late to change our minds."

"And miss all this?"

The music howled, something about someone doing
someone wrong. The crowd shuffled to a halt. Barricades
made of sawhorses and yellow crime-scene tape lay
directly ahead.

Bandit Boy was gone. The man now standing next to
Abi wore a T-shirt with the words "White Power" written in black Magic Marker across his chest. He was a big
man, just beginning to go soft. Beside him, her mother,
the only person left standing between her and the void,
seemed like a frail old lady.

"This is where they search us, I guess."

Leaning on her cane, Alice seemed tired. In the cloudy late-morning light, her wrinkles looked as soft as furrows worn down by rain.

Abi took her arm, but her mother waved her off, growling, "I'm fine, fine."

The crowd waited quietly. People in Indiana were good at waiting for indefinite stretches of time. They did it in companionable silence, with the patience of people who know they'll eventually get what they want—or are resigned to going without. Even the youngest waited well, the two toddlers in their strollers, the teenage boy in the Bob Marley T-shirt.

Directly ahead stood a pair of men maybe four or five years older than her students. They had on baseball caps, and one of them wore a Boilermaker jacket. Purdue Pete glared angrily from the man's back, yellow hammer poised to fall.

"This a beer line?" Purdue Pete was saying. "I'd wait if it was a beer line. This better be good, Lutovsky."

"I'm just curious to see what the hell's going on," Lutovsky answered. "I grew up with them. I partied with those guys."

"See any Black people? I wonder if they'll come. Look at those hippies, man. Hippies love everyone."

"Keep talking like that and your forehead's gonna slope back and your jaw's gonna start jutting out."

A young woman with purple eyeglass frames and dangling yin-yang earrings was passing out fliers. She gave one to Alice, who scanned it and asked, "Who are you with, dear?"

"They'll take away your cane. They'll take away any means you have to fight them."

"Let them try."

The yin-yang woman paused to take Alice's measure. The white and black halves of her earrings—male and female, substance and nothingness—curved into each other like twin fetuses. Abi wondered if she meant to twist the symbol into meaning black and white together, or if she just wore the earrings for fashion's sake.

Yin-Yang Woman was talking to Alice urgently now. The Klan exploited the discontent of working-class whites, she said. To explain unemployment, poverty, and economic insecurity, they scapegoated Jews, Blacks, immigrants, lesbians and gays, and trade unions. People who thought Klan violence was a thing of the past were wrong. They singled out families, usually multiracial ones, to terrorize and make examples of. Just a few years ago, they had killed a young Black man in Ohio.

"Smashed his face in," she said. "What we have to do is smash them back. Join together and smash the Klan."

"Just how do you plan to do that?" said Abi. She scanned her memory for articles about the Ohio Klan killing. Either Yin-Yang Woman was going on rumor or the press had failed to underscore the truth.

Abi's mother patted Yin-Yang's arm. "Keep fighting the good fight, dear," she said, but the woman, holding her fliers high, had already moved ahead through the crowd.

"Empty your pockets," the officer said to the man in the White-Power shirt. "Empty your pockets and raise your hands over your head."

They had reached the head of the line. White-Power Man stood in front of a laminated table, the kind used at church rummage sales. Sucking in his stomach, he reached into his pockets, took out his wallet and keys, and dropped them in the small plastic bucket on the tabletop. When he lifted his arms, the T-shirt rose, exposing his stomach. Black hair curled around his navel. Abi looked up, not wanting to see. Meeting his somber eyes, she blushed and dropped her gaze, surprised that he could actually see her. Somehow, she'd thought she was invisible to him.

A second policeman with a hand-held metal detector passed the thick black wand over White Power's torso. "Turn around, sir," he said. Hands in surgical gloves patted the man's waist and thighs, squeezed his crotch. All the while he stared straight ahead, not at Abi anymore, not at anyone.

"Sir, you may enter," the first officer said. "Please move on."

The man tucked his shirt back into his jeans. He was grinning now. His dark navel under the thin cloth looked like a membrane-covered mouth.

They were next. Since her conversation with Yin-Yang Woman, her mother had drifted off into silence. Abi wondered if her arthritis was acting up again. Sometimes she could almost feel her mother's pain radiate through the air between them, like a ghostly, fevered hand.

"Mom, you OK?"

"Oh, I've been better."

Abi suddenly knew for sure that she couldn't go through with this. The idea of being searched repelled her, but even more she couldn't bear to watch her mother touched by strangers. "Mom," she said, "let's go. We've seen enough. We've *done* enough. Just by virtue of our presence . . ."

"We're almost there. Don't give up now, hon."

"Ma'am," the policeman was saying, not to her mother, to her. "Ma'am, please step up to the line. Empty your pockets. Place your possessions on the table. Small objects go in the bucket."

She unhooked her pouch, then placed it on the card table. His nameplate said "R. A. Largent." R. A. Largent pointed the metal detector at her. His neck was covered with a red rash, bright as a new burn.

"Hands, ma'am. Hands over your head. Higher, please."

A woman officer with short brown hair stepped up behind Abi and began to touch her. The gloved hands patted her arms and underarms, her breasts, waist, groin, and thighs. Numbly, Abi fought to keep her breathing steady. How long since she'd been touched like this? Maybe never. Neither of the men she'd slept with had ever touched her so deliberately, seeking something hidden close to her skin.

"She's OK," the policewoman said.

On the card table in front of her lay two paper clips and some pennies. An ATM receipt. A wallet, keys, a black leather pouch. It took her a second before she realized they were hers.

"This all, ma'am?" R. A. Largent flipped Abi's wallet open, then scanned the rows of ID and credit cards. He was her age, maybe a year or two older. His rash looked chronic, something he'd had to battle his whole life.

"That's all."

His hands under the latex were marbled with baby powder and sweat. In one he held her good fountain pen, which her father had given her for her twenty-first birthday and which she carried with her always.

"You'll have to lose the pen," he said.

"Lose it?"

"Have it confiscated."

"For good?"

"Yes, for good."

"Why?"

"Because it's a potential weapon, ma'am."

Looking at his freckled, open face and brilliant rash, she paused, considering whether or not to argue. Usually, she didn't. Usually she found that when she had to give something up, she didn't miss it once it was gone. This made renunciation easy. During her first weeks in Indiana, she'd searched for feelings of regret, but couldn't find them. She didn't miss her old life, or the friends who, in the months following her father's death, had slipped out of reach. She didn't even miss her father, unless the terrible stillness inside meant missing him.

"Officer Largent, isn't this a bit absurd?"

"Your choice, ma'am. Lose it or leave."

"Largent. Sergeant Largent." Her mother's voice, deep for a woman's, made his name into a song. "You're going to have a rhyming problem when they promote you."

Seeming to relax, to let go for a moment of his role, R. A. Largent grinned. "They call me that already, ma'am."

"Sergeant, the woman you're talking to is my daughter. She's not the type to use any weapon, potential or otherwise. You have a mother's word."

Abi felt her face freeze, although no one was looking at her.

"Ma'am?" R. A. Largent was still smiling, but his smile had grown official.

"Is it my turn yet?" Alice raised her arms in front of her, a stagy sleepwalker's pose, her cane held out like a sword. "If you want me to lift them higher, too bad. That's as far as they go."

Unnoticed, Abi slipped the pen back into her pouch. The wand passed over her mother. The gloved hands touched her, brushed her clipped silver hair, and traveled down her back and arms, over the breasts she no longer kept confined in a brassiere. Her husband's T-shirts were all she ever wore beneath her blouses now. After he'd died, she'd taken to wearing his clothes. In the limbo of the first days of mourning, it had unnerved Abi to come across Alice in the hallway, late at night when neither of them could sleep, dressed in her father's loose robe and boxer shorts, a thatch of gray pubic hair visible through the slit. Only after Abi moved to Lafayette did she realize how she'd braced herself, night after night, against the shock of encountering that double ghost.

"You won't find anything," Alice said now, "only a body that's seen better days."

R. A. Largent gently pried the cane from her hand. "This has to go," he said.

"How's a woman to walk?"

"Your choice, ma'am." He upended her purse, spilling its contents onto the table. Change rang down. Various objects, some familiar, some strange, lay scattered over the simulated wood surface. Abi recognized the Elvis key chain she'd given her last Mother's Day, a bird whistle, a stapler, a tube of Super Glue. A single leather glove, soft as butter, slid out and drooped over the mound. The Spaldings bounced onto the street. R. A. Largent crouched down. When he stood up again, he was holding both balls in one hand. They were the color that used to be called Flesh, and cupped in his palm they looked testicular, obscene.

"Why are you carrying these, ma'am?"

"You don't want to know."

"It's my business to know."

Alice looked him in the eye. "Well then, Sergeant Largent, you are holding my sanity and my strength. The doctors call it therapy. You may call it whatever you please."

"Ma'am?"

"Tell the truth, do I look dangerous?" She slowly turned. Abi could see she was working hard to hold in the pain. "Go on," her mother said. "Feast your eyes."

They walked slowly, like old companions, arm in arm. Alice's grip was surprisingly strong. Sergeant Largent had let her keep the Spaldings, but he'd confiscated the cane and her supply of pens, pencils, and mace, the Swiss Army knife, her flashlight, fold-up umbrella, and travel sewing kit. "The means by which I defend and keep myself together," Alice joked. "A necessary sacrifice, I suppose. Too bad about that umbrella, though, because these bones tell me it's going to rain."

Several hundred people ringed by riot police milled around in front of the courthouse. Some carried torn-up bedsheets with slogans painted on them. "NO MORE INTOLERANCE," one read.

"You live in an astonishing world," her mother was saying. "There's this mess"—she raised her chin toward the courthouse, the crowd, the Plexiglas shields—"but you also have cops who are too sweet and dumb to know when they're being insulted. 'Sergeant Largent.' Bless his soul!"

The amplified music swirled into a tune Abi recognized. It was "Dixie"—no, "The Star-Spangled Banner." The electric guitar soared jaggedly with the high notes, in imitation of Hendrix, then went silent.

"You know what 'Largent' means, don't you?" Alice said. "'L'argent.' Have you forgotten all your French? Think."

"I give up."

"'Money.' His name means 'money.' It's possible he doesn't even know."

"Maybe." Abi had stopped listening. Scanning the crowd, she saw only one African American, a tall young man wearing a Notre Dame baseball cap. Right up against the barricade was a Japanese teenager with wire-rimmed glasses and spiked Barbie-blond hair.

"You'd be surprised how many people don't know the meaning of their own names."

Abi nodded, annoyed with her for going on about nothing at a time like this. As far as she could see, the Black man and Japanese boy were, besides herself, the only ones in the crowd whose skin declared them. The irony of the situation was almost funny. In terms of identity politics, she had resisted being named, as if naming might limit her. If anyone asked, she answered, "Amerasian," a label vague enough to allow her some breathing room. Her identity was nobody's business but her own.

But now her father was dead, and she was trapped in a world where color meant everything—a white world in the landlocked middle of North America in the year 2001. A white *male* world, to judge by the crowd of men in caps and jackets that spelled out the names of their teams, unions, and lodges. These were the men who worked for Caterpillar, Wabash National, or Subaru-Isuzu, the farmers who guided combines over the endless fields, then waited for rain and a good harvest and a decent price for their corn or soybeans or whatever it was they grew. The problem was she couldn't read them. Because of their whiteness, they could be for either side, or no side at all. From the moment she had become aware of racism—truly aware, an awareness that burned into her marrow and gave her the vision to see half-buried signs everywhere—she knew herself to be surrounded by strangers who could hate her to death or just as easily turn into friends.

"You worry too much, Abigail." Her mother spoke slowly, as if her words contained an important truth she'd been waiting for the right moment to reveal. Chuckling, she clutched Abi's arm tighter. "No one would dare mess with a mean old lady like me. Just let them try."

The White-Power man stood near the gleaming shields, talking to seven or eight people who looked like bikers, like older, faded versions of the neo-punk kids who found their way to the streets of the East Village each summer.

Despite the damp chill, some of the men in the group had taken their shirts off. The women rolled up their sleeves and pants legs. They looked weirdly naked among the windbreakers and jackets, like dingy ascetics, damaged saints. Abi's eyes were drawn to the discolorations on their bodies, which from a distance could have been bruises or mud. It took her a moment to see that they were tattoos: a bald eagle, a spider web, a cross. The figure of a hooded Klansman on a horse covered one woman's calf. The scalp of the man next to her was inscribed with a swastika, which glowed under the shaved stubble like a green vein.

Swastika Man said something, and White Power laughed.

"Look!" Alice called. "Skinheads!"

"Sh! They'll hear."

"What if they do?"

Heart beating hard, Abi steered her mother away from them. Spotting Yin-Yang Woman's purple glasses, she headed straight for her. The women with the strollers were there, too. Maybe they'd be safer surrounded by other women. It was worth a try.

"Looks like it might clear. Then again, might not."

The calm, measured voice belonged to a silver-haired woman who wore a wool car coat so vibrantly blue it seemed to give off light. The woman exuded niceness, the distant kind Abi had learned to distrust. She might have been any of the women she saw at Safeway who waited with unnerving patience instead of reaching across her for the iceberg lettuce.

"This is my granddaughter, Sam. Sam, tell the ladies hello," the woman in blue said to a solemn child whose brown hair was woven into two tight braids. "The Knights of the Ku Klux Klan aren't our kind. They're not good people. I wanted Sam to see, in case she gets any ideas."

So that was it. Nice Lady was On Our Side, and she had singled out Abi and her mother to make her point. Abi cringed, the same inward cringe she felt at English-department parties when she was asked what she thought of Amy Tan and the situation in Tibet. She hoped her mother would cut Nice Lady dead, but instead Alice nodded.

"*Brava!* Good for you." Smiling down at the girl, she said, "Hello, dear."

"She's shy," Nice Lady said.

"That won't last."

"No, it won't."

She and Alice grinned at each other, as if sharing a private joke.

"Elsa," the lady said. "Mrs. Elsa Persson, just like the word 'person' but with two S's instead of one. We're from Shadeland."

"I'm Alice Leong."

Her mother was wearing her Pleasant Smile, which Abi, with a twinge of dismay, now recognized as a Midwestern smile. "This is my daughter, Abigail. She lives in Lafayette. I'm just visiting." Before Abi could deny really living in Indiana, Alice and Mrs. Elsa Persson fell to talking about children and their ways, as if they weren't surrounded by skinheads and hostile strangers, as if the air around them wasn't dangerously charged.

Abi leaned down till she was the same height as the girl named Sam. Her braids were held in place by bands with red plastic balls the size of marbles. She regarded Abi suspiciously. "Tell you a secret," Abi whispered. "I don't want to be here either."

A church bell started to toll. The helicopter circled the courthouse spire like a toy attached by a string. Abi straightened back up. The crowd had grown quiet. It was about to begin.

"New York," Elsa Persson was saying. "New York City. We went there for our fortieth. The kids all chipped in. Those homeless people, what a shame. We saw *Les Misérables* and stayed at a far-too-fancy hotel." She paused. "He can still hear me. The doctors say he's only responding to the sound of a voice, but I know he understands."

Alice clasped Elsa Persson's hand between her own. Her expression was fierce and alive. "What do they know about love?"

A murmur rose.

"They're coming," Mrs. Persson said. "I think I see them. Stay close, Samantha."

The skinheads had their arms held out in Nazi salutes. Yin-Yang Woman shook her raised fist, screamed, "Motherfuckers!" Others in the crowd were shouting, too, pressing close to the barricades and shields. A young man with blond dreds pushed past Abi. "Come down here, you ass-holes! I dare you!" he yelled. The Black man in the Notre Dame cap was there, too, standing very, very still.

Alice stared rapturously ahead. Abi took her hand, hoping she was too caught up in the spectacle to notice how her own trembled.

The Klansmen came walking single file around the courthouse. They had their white robes on. Some wore hoods, the same erect white cones she'd seen in history books and documentaries.

"Look at them, will you?" Elsa Persson said. "Trash, Sam. That's what we call trash."

The Klansmen arranged themselves in rows on the courthouse steps. There were sixteen or seventeen of them, including the two who held the American and Confederate flags. Others held small shields painted with crosses or drops of blood. Wind whipped their robes, plastering them against their legs. Abi glimpsed a black boot, a sneaker, faded denim. Her eyes stung with tears. It felt like the time she'd gazed into the hate-brightened eyes of the Tippecanoe Mall woman, only a hundred times worse.

"Hon, you're hurting me." Abi relaxed her grip. The shouting changed into a chant.

Black and white, unite and fight!
Smash the Klan now!
Black and white, unite and fight!
Smash the Klan now!

A man wearing a red robe and hood that didn't hide his face stepped up to the podium. He tapped the micro-phone. Feedback howled, a thin whine nearly drowned out by the shouting crowd. In the flat voice of a man unused to public speaking, he began to talk about how Mexicans, Orientals, and other foreigners were taking American jobs away from Americans. She had to piece the meaning together, because parts of each sentence were lost to the roar. The words "Aryan" and "natural law" floated to the surface. Now gays were the subject, something about God's retribution through AIDS.

Abi stared at the man, who seemed to fade the longer he spoke. Was this the face of evil?

Yin-Yang Woman climbed onto Dreds's shoulders and shook her fist, leading the chant, which was growing louder. The man in the Notre Dame cap grasped the hand of the woman next to him—a young white woman with a shiny black ponytail—and raised their entwined hands high.

Something about the way they held on said the gesture wasn't only symbolic: they were lovers, they made love. The tears overflowed, streamed down Abi's face. She felt her mother give her hand a squeeze—for reassurance, she thought. But then she felt her arm start to lift. Her mother was raising their joined hands, raising them as high as she could manage, showing everyone, making them into a symbol of what they were.

"Mother!" Snatching her hand away, Abi felt a wave of anger, at who or what she didn't know. The microphone squealed. The red-hooded Klansman stepped back as if stung. Another Klansman, in a hoodless white robe, grabbed the mike. Looping the chord around his wrist like a televangelist or rock star, he lunged forward and yelled: "We love you good white Christian people! We hate all you other scum!"

The answering howls tore through the air. Walking around to the front of the podium, he looked down, seeming to listen. "Well, fuck you back!" With one hand, the microphone hand, he lifted his robe, revealing black jeans and cowboy boots. With the other, he squeezed his crotch.

Abi would later attempt to reconstruct what happened next, but as hard as she tried to slow memory down, to stop time, the way she'd tried to stop time when her father died, the exact moment the alarm sounded and red light flashed, and the blue-green line on the monitor stopped tracing the faint valleys of his pulse, she couldn't do it. The shouting around her rose to a roar. Bodies pushed into her, not in the weary crush of rush-hour subways, but suddenly, hard. A windbreakered back slammed into her face, its black sheen all she could see. Her feet lifted, no longer touching the ground. She was flying, caught up in a tremendous swell. A word formed: mother. Abi reached for her mother—to protect, to be protected—but Alice was gone.

Shields and black helmets flashed. Abi's feet touched down. She staggered but didn't fall. Where was her mother? Someone was weeping. Was it she herself? No, it was the child, Sam, and when Abi reached down to lift her, her body, at first angular, went limp with trust. Her hair smelled like autumn leaves. Although Sam was a solid girl, she felt light, weightless, a nylon-wrapped bundle of bones. The strength Abi possessed was magical. With it she could carry any weight in the world.

Then it was over. Everyone backed away from each other. Sam slid to the ground. Mrs. Persson's hairspray-stiff hair stood out at strange angles, like something broken. Her mother . . .

"Abigail? Hon? Where are you?" Abi turned and gathered her mother into her arms. Pulling back to survey her face, she realized something was wrong. Alice's glasses were gone. Without them, her face seemed naked.

"You OK, Mom?"

"You let go."

"But you're OK?"

"Blind as a bat, but yes, OK. What's happening? Tell me everything," Alice snapped.

"Mom . . ." Abi squatted to retrieve the glasses. The round silver frames were bent, both lens holes empty.

"You're the one with the eyes. Use them."

The shield-bearing police had moved into the crowd and now stood in two rows, back to back, forming a human wall that divided the demonstrators. On the other side stood the skinheads and White-Power Man. His shirt was streaked with dirt, and his hands hung at his sides, palms facing back. He seemed diminished somehow. Staring at his puffy, unhappy face, Abi remembered the strange longing in Alice's voice when, an age ago, before the rally began, she'd said, "Good country people."

Most of the crowd stood on the same side as Abi and her mother. Yin-Yang Woman was there, and so were many of the unreadable men. Two of them held a bedsheet banner that read, KKK MUST GO! / IRONWORKERS LOCAL 379.

Suddenly, the air above filled with shining fragments, like raindrops in a sun shower.

"What? What is it?" Her mother helplessly scanned the sky.

"I don't know."

Money. The crowd was throwing money, handfuls of change. Coins chinged off the marble steps. Some hit their target, denting the Klansmen's robes like late-spring hail. The man with the microphone raised his arms to ward the brightness off.

"Come on," Alice said, "out with it!"

Abi told her.

"How clever!" Alice said. *"L'argent. L'argent de poche.* A weapon. Of course."

Taking Abi's hand in hers, she turned it palm upward, like a fortune teller. While Abi watched, her mother filled it with change.

"Do it. Go on, hon. Do it for us."

Abi closed her hand around the coins, measuring their cool weight. She paused, then, with all her strength, hurled the coins. Losing track of their arc, she couldn't see which ones hit or missed, but it didn't matter. Her mother filled her hand again and again and again. When she finally ran out of change, Abi dug into her own pouch for the pennies and paper clips. When they, too, were gone, lost in the sparkling barrage, her mother rummaged through her purse and pulled out the Spaldings.

The first ball bounced off the steps, but the second glanced off the cowboy-booted Klansman's shin. He didn't seem to notice. His hands were crossed in front of his face.

"I think we got him," Abi said.

"Brava!" The blind eyes glistened. *"Brava,* my dear."

Before they parted ways, Elsa Persson said they must come and visit if they ever found themselves in Shadeland.

"Four and a half miles from the firehouse. We're the big white house on your right. Now tell the nice ladies good-bye, Sam."

Sam gravely nodded. Abi nodded back, then watched them recede into the crowd.

"Where's the pen I saved you?" Alice said. "Write that down. Never forget when someone tells you how to find them."

And now a few large raindrops splattered against the

windshield. Abi switched on the wipers, which smeared the dust into translucent white fans. The sky was dark with fast-moving clouds. Green light glowed on the horizon, washing the silos, fields, and orphaned trees in its weird luminescence. She was exhausted. Her knees ached. She had expected to feel happy and relieved. After all, they'd survived the rally more or less intact. They had taken their stand. She had even let go of ambivalence and tried on courage—tried it on like a cloak flung around her shoulders in the faded mirror of a vintage clothing store. Why, then, this feeling of emptiness?

"I think we turn here," Alice said softly. The map lay crumpled on her lap. She peered over the tops of her old aviators, which she'd found buried at the bottom of her bag.

Suddenly the sky blurred. Rain came sheeting down. Abi turned on the headlights, flipped the wipers from Sporadic to Fast. Even so, the windshield went molten. Squinting, she inched forward. There seemed to be a gravel bib at the side of the road, which she pulled onto.

"We'll have to wait it out."

Abi twisted in her seat to examine her mother. If she felt exhausted, her mother must be tired beyond words.

"Where are we?" Alice asked.

Her upper lip was pursed, which signaled that she was incensed or in serious pain. More alarming was how she seemed to have shrunk, as Abi's father did after the life left his body.

"I don't know," Abi said gently. Peering through the fogged glass, she saw a solitary train car. Blue and red neon glowed in one of the windows, but she couldn't read the sign.

"I think it's a diner, Mom."

"Grand. You must be famished, and I have to pee like nobody's business."

"Let's wait it out."

"No, hon. It could go on like this for Lord only knows how long."

Her mother rummaged in her bag and pulled out a plastic rain bonnet, folded like an accordion. "Here," she said. Before Abi could take it or protest, she swung the car door open. In rushed the cold green scent of rain. Entering the storm was like sinking into a deep lake. Blinking back the drops, Abi ran to her mother, who was already standing, and tried to plaster the rain bonnet over her head. When that failed, Abi took off her soaked jacket and held it over her.

Although it was only a few steps to the diner, by the time they got there, they were drenched. The door opened into a vestibule. Over the interior door was a bas-relief bald eagle, its talons curled around a sheaf of arrows. Abi guided her mother under the eagle, into the fluorescence.

Smoke hung thick near the ceiling. The murmuring voices stopped. The men in the booths facing away from the door turned to watch. Somebody coughed.

"Where's the bathroom?" Abi asked. One beat passed, then two. The woman behind the counter nodded to the right. "Over there."

Abi sat in the empty booth near the rest rooms. Although it was in the middle of nowhere, the diner was full. Most of the customers were men in green, blue, or orange coveralls. They turned back to their coffee, cigarettes, and meals. The loudest sound was the clink of silverware.

When Alice finally emerged from the women's room,

Abi gestured around the diner and said, "What do you think?"

"Lovely." Her mother's voice was vacant. The unsmiling waitress, who wore a white pantsuit like a nurse, set two plastic menus on the table. "Regular or decaf?" she said.

"Regular, please."

"Decaf," Alice murmured.

Without another word, the waitress walked away. Glancing at her mother, Abi was filled with a helplessness she was afraid to name. The waitress's coolness, if that's what it was, would have been ordinary in a coffee shop in New York, but here it bore a different meaning. Abi was tired of having to guess. She had shared a shining moment of solidarity, but now the uncertainty was starting all over again. She was sick to death of living among these taciturn people who held their true selves so deeply inside she knew almost nothing about them. Suddenly, she was gripped by the desire to tell her mother everything, tell her before it was too late—tell her all about the woman at the mall and the white Christian males, and the scowls and forced smiles, and how lonely she felt, and angry, and sorry, too: sorry she had moved to her mother's Dark Heartland where she'd been made aware, for the first time in her life, of the distance between them.

Alice held up a prescription bottle. "Hon," she said, "do me a huge favor and open this."

The cap wasn't childproof. A drop of water slid down the side of Alice's face to her chin. Using the paper napkin that enfolded her silverware, Abi reached across the table and gently patted her mother's cheek dry.

The waitress returned with two coffeepots. Setting one down, she upended the thick white mugs on the table. "Use these to dry off with. I swiped them from the kitchen," she said, handing Abi the two clean dishtowels tucked under her arm.

"Why, thank you," Alice said, brightening.

The waitress smiled. "You ladies ready, or do you need more time?"

Abi looked at her mother's hands, the knobbed, fragile wrists. "More time," she said.

The edges of the towels were decorated with a pattern of geese and blue hearts. Alice draped hers around her neck, like a boxer after a fight. Squinting over her aviators at the menu, she said, "I'm afraid you'll have to translate, hon."

Deluxe Burger Plate. American fries. Biscuits and gravy. Alice grinned. "Dear God," she said, "sausage gravy, no doubt. Have I ever told you the test of good gravy? It has to be so thick you can stand a spoon in it."

Sounds drifted around them: metal on china, the low murmur of talking men, rain.

"White food." Alice shook her head, smiling. "White food for white people."

The waitress came over, pad in hand. "Whatever you do, save room for dessert. Annie made raspberry cobbler this morning, and her cobbler's famous around here."

When she was gone, Alice leaned across the table. "So," she said, "what did you think of the face of evil?"

Abi thought of the work boots under the robes, of White-Power Man's sagging jowls.

"Pretty banal," she said at last.

"Yes, that's the terrible part. Its ordinariness."

Their lunches arrived, a cheeseburger for Abi, a Smart-Heart special for her mother. Together they gazed at Alice's plate, at the wedge of iceberg lettuce doused with bright orange dressing, and at the twin mounds of cottage cheese, each topped with a maraschino cherry.

"Served without an ounce of irony," Abi said at last.

"None at all."

"White food . . ."

". . . for a white woman."

Abi began to laugh hilariously, as if laughter was what she'd been holding back all this time. Her mother joined in, laughing so hard she had to remove her glasses and dab at her tears with her dishtowel. The men sitting close to them turned to watch. For once, Abi didn't care.

"'Does this make me a racist?'" she recited. "'I think not. There is a conspiracy . . .'"

"And we're in on it," Alice said. The blue eyes dimmed, and Abi knew sad tears were next, but for once she didn't steel herself against them. *Laughter and resistance. Sorrow.* Two sides of the same coin. Why had it taken her this long to see?

"Your father . . ." Alice spoke softly, as if she was lost. "Your father would have been so proud."

"Glad you ladies are having such a good time," the waitress said. She set another plate on the table. A fragrant red stain, dark as blood, seeped through the whipped cream. "I took the liberty," she said. "I knew you'd want some, and this was the last piece."

"You read our minds," Abi said.

"Where you ladies from?"

Abi paused. "My mother's visiting from New York. I'm from Lafayette."

"Right down the road," the waitress said. "You come back then, come back real soon. Tuesday is catfish night."

As promised, the cobbler was delicious, crumbling and sweet. "A saving grace," Alice said.

"Let's go home, Mom," Abi said. "Rest."

"Yes."

Abi paid the bill, which the waitress delivered on a small tray with two sunburst mints. Although rain still pounded down, the sky shimmered with dark silver light.

"Ready?"

"How about you?" Alice asked her. "Are you?"

Abi felt the stillness well up again, only now she knew its name.

Her mother folded the soaked dishtowel once, twice, then slowly rose. Rising, too, Abi took her arm. This time she didn't resist.

THE CHILDREN

∽

The dead boy's shrine lay no more than a few paces from my grandmother's kitchen, but if you looked out the kitchen window, you couldn't see it. The window was wide enough, and it framed the right view—the rosaries, flowers, and other mementos left at the fence—but the shrine was obscured by the slats of the venetian blinds my aunt May always kept tilted half closed. Brown plastic bags, the kind you get from the supermarket, were stuffed into the cracks between the sash and pane. If this wasn't enough, pots of overgrown red chrysanthemums lined the sill. My grandmother loved chrysanthemums. She used to love them for their color and life. After the first stroke, she loved them for the faces of the children she saw in the flowers and leaves.

That afternoon, the three of us, my grandmother, May, and I, sat in the kitchen, not because we were eating—we weren't—but because it was the warmest room in the house. May told me they were conserving fuel. Then she said the dead boy's girlfriend wanted to keep candles burning on the spot where he fell, which by an ugly stroke of fate was right outside the chain-link fence that enclosed my grandmother and aunt's narrow side yard.

"Can you imagine?" May said.

I didn't know exactly what she meant, but I nodded. Looking into her eyes, I couldn't help noticing the angry bruises of insomnia underneath. When my grandmother got up each night to wander, May rose, too, long black hair hanging loose around her shoulders, and followed her through a house rife with danger: steep stairs, rings of fire, linoleum worn slick as ice.

May wanted to tell the whole story, and who was I to stop her. The police really *did* outline the boy's body in chalk, but it rained, then there was that big snowstorm, and by the time the snow melted, the outline was gone. What remained were the beads and crosses, the letters, photographs, and artificial flowers—roses, mostly—whose stems twined like living vines around the steel links. Mourners kept adding to the shrine. May never caught them at it, but each time she left the house, there was something new. A tiny artificial Christmas wreath. A key chain with a miniature basketball attached. Mounds of candle wax glazed the masonry, like stalagmites rising from the floors of caves.

Saying I looked cold, May handed me an afghan, a cro-cheted splash of clashing colors. She was in the middle of describing how troublesome the dead boy's friends and family had been.

"The mother and the girlfriend actually came to see me," she said. "I told them the shrine was their business, they could keep it as long as they wanted. But not the candles, not with all the trash and leaves flying around. They could go up in flames, then where would we be?"

For some reason, the urgent note in her voice embarrassed me. I nodded, Go on.

"The girlfriend hooked her fingers into the fence. She

wouldn't let go. The mother couldn't get to her move. Luckily, a teacher from the high school was there, and he managed to calm her down. 'The ladies are thinking of the fire hazard,' he told her. 'You've got to think of the fire hazard, too.'"

I thought of my grandmother's house, surrounded by pine trees and unpruned hydrangeas, a forgotten patch of forest in the middle of Queens. Before I could push the image away, flames exploded through the branches, licked the windows, feathered the eaves.

"The teacher kept repeating the girl's name, which sounded like Loopy. 'Loopy, Loopy, come on, baby, let's go.' Loopy, Loopy, over and over. As if he was trying to remind her who she was."

My aunt paused. She looked at my grandmother, who was sitting in the straight-backed chair by the refrigerator staring at me, shifting her gaze from me to the chrysanthemums and back again, as she had since I arrived.

"You okay, Ma?" All urgency was gone. Her voice was soft and patient now.

My grandmother wore the angora sweater I bought her last Christmas. A green penumbra of fuzz radiated from her thin arms.

"The children are happy to see you," she said.

"I don't see any children, Ma," May said gently.

"They don't say much, but they're happy. You know how kids are."

"I don't see any children," May said again.

"They're shy around people they haven't seen in a long, long time. But they'll get used to you."

May glanced at me, to gauge how I was taking this. Although I'd been forewarned, a wave of feeling rushed through me, fast and incomplete, like the ripped-to-shreds dreams you have in the weird sleep of general anesthesia. Ever since she came back from the hospital last summer, my grandmother, who'd slowly faded for years, saw things only she could see. At times her visions were surreal: a woman with flowers that blossomed from her shoulders and neck; another woman trapped inside a box, with her head and arms sticking through. Most often, though, she saw children. They lived under the table and among the chrysanthemums. They whispered, ran, hid in the basement behind the stacks of *National Geographics* and boxes of roots and herbs from my grandfather's old store. May said the children were Black or Chinese, depending, and that my grandmother talked to them and worried over them. She didn't know where they came from, but she understood they'd been abandoned.

Two bobby pins held my grandmother's white-streaked hair away from her face. She looked at me expectantly. I didn't know how to answer, so I smiled. Her eyes moved from side to side, down and up, as if she was trying to focus, read me, in English and in Chinese. She seemed dazed, love struck, and I found myself longing for the time when her gaze was as clean as a knife.

Turning to May, I said, "What happened? Tell me from the start."

"All right," she said slowly. "I heard the shots. By the time I got to the window, he was already on the ground. At first I thought it was a car backfiring or some kids lighting off M-80s, then people started running over from the high school. I went outside, but didn't go past the gate. A man yelled, 'Call 911, call 911!' so I ran back inside."

"Did my grandmother see?" The moment the words left my mouth, I realized I was using the language of absence, although she was sitting right there.

"You see anything, Grandma?"

Her eyes drifted back to the chrysanthemums. The bottom leaves were dry and brown, but the rust red flowers still smelled pungently fresh.

"No," said May, "I don't think she did."

My grandmother blinked. Understanding seemed to dawn. "Are you hungry? Did you eat?"

"You want a sandwich?" May asked. "There's some turkey and some Swiss cheese. Sorry, but it's all low fat, low salt."

"Low everything," my grandmother said.

Clementines and hazelnut cookies, my offering, lay untouched on two chipped Wedgwood platters. In better days, when my grandmother's eyes were like knives and her black hair was marcelled so smooth it looked like oil or ink, when my grandfather was still alive and my parents and brothers and sisters and I visited every weekend, the same kitchen table was covered with platters of *bao* and sliced red pork, and the *baci*, little kisses, that my grandmother's Chinatown friends brought from Little Italy. Now it was laden with old magazines and bills, her medicines, and the family-size boxes of raisin bran and corn flakes that came from the woman next door. My aunt and the neighbor, who was from Taiwan, swapped commodity cereal for bags of rice. The neighbor received the cereal—which to her was bizarre and inedible—through Aid to Families with Dependent Children. "She doesn't understand corn flakes," my grandmother once explained. "Real Chinese don't drink milk."

"No, thanks," I told May, "I had a late breakfast. Please. I'm fine."

She leafed through the top newspapers on one of the waist-high piles of newspapers near the window, then passed a handful of clippings to me. The *Daily News*, the *Post*, the *Times*. Although I didn't say so, I was surprised the murder had attracted so much attention. In *Newsday*, there was a photograph of the street outside the kitchen window. It took me a moment to understand that the grainy image of an anonymous brick house surrounded by an anonymous chain-link fence was, in fact, my grandmother's. More than the shrine outside the window, the sting of recognition made the crime seem real.

Among the uniformed officers were two plainclothesmen in raincoats, one of whom held a Styrofoam cup with steam rising from its mouth. Crime-scene tape stretched from the fence post to the stop sign on the corner. I could actually make out the words, SCENE DO NOT CROSS CRIME SCENE DO NOT.

Beneath that photo was a studio portrait of a kid with close-cropped hair. He was Black—no, Latino. Jason P. Veracruz. Jason P. Veracruz wore a tuxedo. He looked younger than sixteen, the number that followed his name. Scanning the first few paragraphs, I discovered that he was a popular student, a member of the debate team. On the afternoon he died, he left school to buy an orange soda and a bag of potato chips, and was on his way back when he was shot twice in the abdomen and once in the neck, the fatal wound. According to the police, he was killed because he refused to give up his gold chain.

The reason for the media attention was now clear. The story of Jason Veracruz's death was a chapter in a book of stories so similar they could all be the same: a nice kid, a senseless death over a chain, a jacket, a pair of athletic shoes. The moral of the story had something to do with devalued lives and the times, and how terrible the city was, but sitting in my grandmother's cold kitchen that winter afternoon, I couldn't think of morals. Everything fell apart.

"I talked to the reporters, but first I made them swear not to use my name," May said. "I talked to the cops, too. I guess that makes me a witness, even if I told them over and over I didn't see anything."

The last light angling through the blinds striped the dusty chrysanthemums. I wondered what May *did* see. How had she occupied herself all those hours while police and reporters milled outside the house measuring, drinking coffee, taking pictures, making notes, taping their words of warning across the fence?

That winter, May was forty-nine. The youngest daughter, she never left home. For ages, it seemed, she tended to my ailing grandfather, traveling with him over the long, slow arc that led to his death a dozen years ago. May was forty-nine, but with her black hair and smooth skin, she could have been my sister. She was wearing jeans, a sweatshirt, and Frye boots, her usual uniform. In the days when they still had visitors, someone, somebody white, asked why she always wore boots, and she said, "Because my feet are bound."

She rarely went out, only to shop at Key Food or to take my grandmother to the doctor. I have to admit that her behavior didn't seem that strange—except in those rare, awful moments when I stopped to think about the situation. Then my grandmother and aunt changed shape before the eye of memory. They swelled, grew distorted, became the women you heard about in another, older volume of stories: the shut-ins, recluses, the witches nobody sees. The hand that lifts the curtain and lets it fall back into place.

"The children are frightened," my grandmother was saying.

"Frightened?"

"People yell at them and hit them for no reason. You can't blame them for being scared."

With a guilty start, I realized she'd been listening all along.

"They have suspects," May said, "but I'm not going to testify, not in a million years. Those guys have to be crazy, shooting that kid like that, in broad daylight. They're crazy, and crazy people can do anything. Like burn down a house."

"They won't burn the house down."

"How do you know?"

"They won't."

"You don't think." It wasn't a question. May looked toward the window, and I followed her eyes. "That fucking shrine," she said.

My breath stopped, but my grandmother was staring off into space.

"The shrine's like an arrow pointing at us, saying it happened here, *this* is the place."

Her voice had grown almost loud, louder than I'd ever heard it before.

"It says *this, this, this! This* is the house where somebody died."

My heart was beating so hard I could feel the pulse in my throat. If she said another word, we would implode, wrapped in flames.

May stared at her hands, which gripped her knees. I groped for the right comforting words, anything to keep her from talking, from declaring what had welled up inside her for years.

"Don't worry, they'll forget," I said. "When the shrine

comes down, they'll forget. People have short memories these days."

Silence told me I'd said the wrong thing. May glared, then turned away. After a moment she began to pack my hazelnut cookies back into their box. Before I knew it, she had wrapped and retied the box with the red string from the bakery.

"Take them with you," she murmured, her voice shrunk back to normal. "We don't eat this kind of stuff anymore. Take them, so they won't go to waste."

She was smiling, but I kept seeing the glare she gave me the moment before, the bitter eyes that said, *How do you know? How do you know anything?*

A half hour later, my grandmother leaned toward May and said something in Cantonese. May nodded, then told me I should go before it got too dark. Relieved and sad, I folded the afghan and placed it on top of the newspapers. When I kissed my grandmother's cheek, I breathed in her dry, old woman's smell, the acrid scent of chrysanthemums.

The time came to kiss my aunt. Her face softened a little. "Take care of yourself, kiddo."

"I'll be back soon."

"It's good to see you," my grandmother said. "It's always good." She tried to tuck something into my hand, a folded bill, a five. She must have been holding it all along, through the hours I sat with them both.

"No, Grandma, don't."

"Take it. Just take it," said May.

Before I fully understood how I got there, I was out past the pine trees, the hydrangeas. The air was sharp and cold. Twenty-five years ago, when my brothers and

sisters and I were children, we helped May bury steel
wool around the roots, to bring color to the flowers. I
never knew if we were responsible for the pale blue, or if it
was just an idea we had. May's hair gleamed in schoolgirl
braids, and now I remembered the odor of damp earth,
the cold, gritty feel of it under my nails.

It was starting to snow. I swung the gate open. When
I looked back at the kitchen window, the light was on.
My grandmother and May peered through the venetian
blinds. All I saw were two dark forms, one taller than the
other. I waved, wondering what they could see. Someone
had set out three new votive candles and lighted them.
The flames roared softly in the wind.

SAFETY

⌒

Finally I said, "OK, I give up, let's do it," so the following Saturday, Luke took me to see his friend Paul so I could learn how to shoot and, if need be, kill.

At the edge of Paul's property, near the fence that marked the beginning of the red wilderness shimmering between our valley and the Sangre de Cristos, was a natural sandstone amphitheater. The three of us—my lover, his buddy, and the neophyte, the city girl, me—stood within its crescent of shade. Because it was June, the hottest month of the year, before the onset of the cooling monsoons, we'd held off my lesson until it was almost dusk. When I asked if there would be enough light to see by, Paul grinned.

"Are you kidding, Angel?" he said. "We're talking the perfect balance. Bright and dark together, like man and woman, yin and yang."

Two bats or swallows—I didn't know how to tell them apart back then—darted across the deep blue sky. Paul looked down while he spoke, the way old-fashioned Spanish men did when they wanted to show respect for a strange woman, but his smile was anything but respectful. Usually I knew how to deal with his kind. Cool silence worked best; it left them with nothing to hang onto. But

Paul had stopped smiling. Lifting his eyes, he swung his long blond hair away from his face, then handed me the shotgun.

"Try this on for size," he said.

My arms dipped under the weight. The thing was much heavier than I'd imagined. I steadied myself, but not before Paul and Luke exchanged knowing glances, their faces free for a moment—a moment only—from the animated, almost angry expression that certain men wore around me when I was young. Without their masks, they looked calm and older. Serious. I sensed I had glimpsed them as they really were.

"This is how you hold one of these babies." Paul guided the butt into the hollow place in my shoulder. The stock was made of densely grained wood, the barrel of metal so black it absorbed the light. His knuckles brushed my breast, too slow a touch to be entirely accidental. I peered at Luke, but he either hadn't seen or was pretending not to.

Luke was the man I was with that summer, and Paul was his best friend. We were all neighbors in El Porvenir, the name given to a few houses scattered along a bend in the Porvenir River. Fifteen years earlier, Luke had moved to New Mexico after college, as I had the year before; but unlike me, who'd wandered there with vague ideas of adventure, his reason was to disappear after his birth date had drawn a low number in the lottery. "You wouldn't believe it, Tess. Seven," he'd told me. "Only time I've ever been lucky." Northern New Mexico was home to a fair number of draft dodgers, he said. It was as close as you could get to leaving the country without actually crossing any borders, and I think that was what drew me to him: how close he seemed to the edge.

Paul was more mysterious. All I really knew about him was that he had completely restored the hundred-year-old adobe house where he'd lived with his wife and little daughter, and where he now lived alone. He had a past, but nobody was supposed to talk about it. One of the few things Luke told me about him was that he was good with his hands. Both men were in their mid-thirties, which seemed old to me then, and both were Anglos who'd scratched out an existence in Northern New Mexico for so long that the lilt of a Spanish accent had seeped into their voices, and I couldn't imagine them living anywhere else.

Paul may have been Luke's best friend, but from the very start he came on to me.

"What an angel. Where'd you find her, *cabrón?*"

The Saturday I first met him, about a month earlier, Luke was helping Paul reroof his house. While they worked, I sat in the shade and sipped watery black coffee. I hadn't wanted to come, but Luke had said it was high time I'd met his buddy. Besides, they needed me for inspiration.

They were drinking beer, had a cooler up on the roof with them. The air was thick with the reek of hot tar. The two men, both wiry-strong and tan, seemed almost interchangeable, one pale haired, one dark. Listening to them talk about their work and about a truck Paul was thinking of buying, I wouldn't have taken them for anything but local men whose families had lived in the valley for hundreds of years. If this was a disguise, the kind of mask outsiders can wear in a place that does not welcome them, then it was grafted to the flesh.

Dogs barked. A distant chain saw whined. I felt restless and unsure of my purpose. A large orange cat ran into

the open shed. Glad to have something to fix my attention on, I called up to the roof to ask its name.

"Asshole," Paul said. "His name is Asshole."

"No, really."

"It's true. Once upon a time could be he had another
name, but that's history. Asshole's the name he comes to
now. He doesn't care, so long as he gets fed."

I gazed up at the roof, but could only see the sun.

"Come here, Angel. I want to show you something,"
Paul said.

"I'm not your angel."

"Who said you were? Come here."

When I walked warily over, shading my eyes against
the glare, Paul turned to Luke, who was smoothing liquid
tar over the surface with a blackened broom. "She been
good?" he asked.

"Good enough."

Paul leaned down and slipped a cool, sweating bottle
into my hand. At first he was a dark outline of himself,
then gradually I could distinguish him. His blond braids
were bound together across his chest with a strip of raw-
hide, the way I'd seen Taos and Plains Indian men bind
theirs. He didn't have a shirt on, and that's when I noticed
he was missing a nipple—no scar, just smooth skin where
the left nipple should have been. When I asked Luke
about it later, and he muttered something about a construction accident, I thought I could sense a lie concealing
a darker cause. "OK," I'd said. "So how exactly did it happen?" "How exactly?" Luke echoed. "Zip. Zip, zap, that's
how we lose everything the goddess gave us."

Something soft brushed my leg: Asshole, the cat. I
lifted my eyes from Paul's chest to his face, but it was too

late, he had seen me look. Grinning, he turned back to his work.

If I had never encountered Paul again, he might have lived in my imagination, if he lived at all, as the image of a slightly dangerous man with an interesting wound. But the story didn't end there because Luke became obsessed with the idea of getting me armed, and Paul was a man with weapons to spare.

The campaign began when Luke found the knife under my bed. At the time, we were just beginning to get serious, if that's what we were. I was still getting used to the feel of him—his long, thin body, the dark cloud of hair at the base of his spine, his expansive moods, when he could hold forth for hours, and his quietness, too, when he'd draw into himself or literally disappear, sometimes for days. At first I'd thought he was with another woman, till he'd told me not to worry, he only went off from time to time to lick his wounds.

The night he'd found the knife, I had returned from the bathroom to see him sitting cross-legged on the bed. Something in his hand glinted. My secret weapon.

"What do you call this?"

Only three inches long, the blade was honed sharp enough to slice a hair. I wondered how he'd found it, if he'd groped among the dust balls and books, and whatever else had collected under the cinder-block-raised boards.

Luke was smiling. It was the same smile he wore when he called me city girl or chided me about the fancy school I'd gone to and my job as a reporter for the *Rio Bravo Sun*, as if that gave me the right to stake a claim in a place like

El Porvenir and write about the people who really lived there.

Passing my knife from one hand to the other, he said, "I'm waiting. What do you call this?"

"A knife."

He tapped the flat of the blade on his palm. "Try again."

"OK," I said, "I call it protection."

"That's what I was afraid of. Protection from what, I wonder?" He passed my knife from hand to hand again, and the blade and his teeth and the white scar on his thigh shone in the candlelight. "Tess, you're even more deluded than I thought if you believe in this toy. Know how easy it'd be to turn against you?" His smile began to fade. "A paring knife. What do you want to do? Peel the guy's apples? Think."

I already had. Even though I'd never been attacked, I had imagined it, had seen myself startled out of sleep by the sound of breaking glass. I knew how easy a target I was, living alone. My nearest neighbors were my land-lords, the Luceros, whose house a hundred yards up the hill was separated from mine by a stand of cottonwoods and thorny Russian olive trees. Back then, I wasn't afraid of things that by all rights should have terrified me. In fact, I was so unafraid that now it seems grace alone kept me alive. But I was afraid of this: of being broken into where I was most vulnerable. I couldn't endure the thought of being helpless. At the time, it was the most terrifying fate I could imagine.

The night the man intruded into my world, I was sitting at the kitchen table reading the *Sun*. After seven months at the newspaper, the presence of my byline, my printed name, still amazed me. Every Wednesday, the day the *Sun* came out, I would read my words one last time, thrilled by how public and final they'd become. I'd found that I loved reporting. All I had to do was ask questions, and most people answered. Most people, I discovered, weren't used to being listened to. Out of gratitude, it seemed, they would tell me their deepest secrets. Because of my ambiguous, dark-haired looks, they may have thought I resembled a native New Mexican enough to be worthy of trust. Using the disguise I'd been born with, I pulled the stories out of them. The power I held astonished me.

The kitchen window was no more than three feet from where I sat. In retrospect I could say that I felt myself being watched. In any event, something made me look up, and when I looked, I saw the man's disembodied head floating in the darkness. His skin was very pale. He had dark eyes with thin eyebrows, and when he saw that I had seen him, he kept on staring. His expression remained neutral: no, not neutral—completely blank. I screamed. When I opened my eyes again, he was still there, as if to show me he felt no need to run, he could take his time. A second later, he was gone.

I spent that night at the Luceros. While Lia made up the bed in their youngest son's old room, Joe went into their bedroom and came out again with a revolver. "It's a .22. Nice size for a lady." His hazel eyes gleamed with amusement when I turned him down. My refusal told him I was a crazy Anglo after all. I must have sounded even crazier when I tried to explain how I was more afraid of possessing a gun than of the danger it was meant to protect me from.

Afterward I slept with my sharp little knife, but it was too late, the nights had come alive. The wind spoke, dogs howled their warnings. I saw the man's face at every window. It became my bad dream, the full moon that wrecked sleep. His blank stare was what scared me the most. The look he'd given me was the same one you might give a small animal trapped in a cage. It told me he knew he didn't have to respond to me, that I was as good as unconscious or dead. That I was at his mercy.

"Give me my knife," I said to Luke.

"No way." He put both hands behind his back. "I'm doing you a favor. I'm saving your life."

"Give it to me."

"No."

With his hands held behind him like a handcuffed prisoner, he looked almost happy. He had a mission. Whether I liked it or not, he was going to rescue me. He was going to get me a real weapon and see that I learned how to use it.

I lunged. He laughed. "Just you wait," he said. It was then I remembered I barely knew him. He was still a stranger, and an unpredictable stranger at that. *A loser.* The words rose up out of nowhere, but right away I knew they were true. That was the first time I had thought of Luke as someone who could be written off, and for a second I felt guilty, as if he could read my mind.

The shotgun was growing heavier. I felt nervous holding it without instructions about what to do. Then Paul came up behind me. Putting his arms around me, hands over my hands, he guided my finger to a tiny silver button on the stock. "The safety," he said.

His breath was warm, even warmer than the air. I glanced at Luke, who was leaning against a boulder, thoughtfully peeling the foil from the mouth of his Dos Equis. He'd untied his ponytail, and his hair hung in a dark, torn curtain around his face. He seemed calm, but

I knew enough by now to be suspicious, because in him calmness could blossom into anger.

"Here's the most important lesson you'll ever learn," Paul said. "This means the safety's on." He made my finger circle the button and push down. "This means off. On, off. On," he said. "Off. Got it?"

"I'm not stupid."

"No one said you were. Get so you know it by heart, so that it's like instinct. Always always *always* keep the safety on, until you're sure you're ready to fire. Understand?"

"Of course."

"The second you click it off, follow through. You're committed. It's like a promise you've made to the asshole who wants to do you harm. He hears that safety click, he knows you're serious. And you'd better be."

He ran my finger over the button. "So which is it? On or off?"

I thought for a moment. "Off."

"That's right, Angel. Ready?"

A breeze lifted my hair. In it I smelled the unseen river, the one that had, over thousands of years, carved the Porvenir Valley out of its bed of volcanic stone. I thought of the nippleless smooth half of Paul's chest, so strange yet lovely, too, the way I'd imagined the ideal human body should be when I was a kid, the sleek flow of skin uninterrupted by navels, birthmarks, or blemishes of any kind. Did I want him? I couldn't tell. My arms were tired, and I wanted to finish this business so I could lower them, but I was afraid of the explosion, the violence, the noise. I was afraid—I can say this now—that I would like it.

"I don't know," I said.

"What don't you know?"

"I don't know if I can do this."

Chuckling, he released me. Unsupported by his arms, mine sagged under the shotgun's weight. Gingerly, I clicked the safety back on.

Paul turned to Luke. "Where'd you get this girl?"

"Better ask her."

"Let's take a break," Paul said. *"Cabrón,* pass your brother another beer."

"I'll have one, too."

Getting up, Luke drew a bottle out of the cooler and gave it to Paul. "Not till you've earned it."

"Come on." I tried to touch his arm, but he flinched, then took the shotgun away from me.

"What do you want to do?" Luke muttered. With one smooth gesture, which I now knew to admire, he lifted the shotgun and took aim. Shoulders hunched, he looked so angry and sad that I felt a surge of tenderness, as if I had wronged him.

"Top of that tree," he said. "The dead one over there."

The blast tore the stillness open. My closed eyelids quivered. My heart clenched, its wet fist squeezed tight. Although I'd lived most of my life in the city, surrounded by noise, I had never heard anything so loud so close before. Pile drivers, sirens, jackhammers. . . . Even the accident I'd witnessed, a cab slamming broadside into another cab, was a strangely muted event, the thud-crunch followed by a trough of quietude before the shouting and blood began.

When I opened my eyes again, smoke drifted in a thin haze. The smell of sulfur was oddly pleasing.

"Not bad, *ese,*" Paul said.

"See?" Luke said softly, to me. "You just pull the fucking trigger. It's not so hard. Now stop wasting our time."

"Your precious time."

If we had been alone, the fighting would have started

in earnest. Within a few minutes, the battle would have escalated to the point where we'd be yelling. After I had spent myself, he would smile coldly and name my flaws. When he'd finished wearing me down, he would take me in his arms and we'd make love. But we weren't alone. Paul was standing right there. I felt a stab of delicious shame, as if he had watched us take off our clothes and enter into the first delirious kiss.

"Now children, no arguing. We're one big happy family," Paul said.

Luke eyed him cautiously. "Whatever you say, bro."

"Angel," Paul said, "I think you're ready for round two."

This time, although he stood close enough to whisper, he didn't touch me. I thought I'd feel uneasy holding the shotgun alone, but I didn't. Maybe it wasn't as heavy as I'd remembered. Maybe I had imagined all that weight.

"Tell you a secret," Paul said. "See this place, this hillside? Before . . ." He trailed off. "Before, when it wasn't just me and the fucking cat, I used to come up here to be alone."

Shadows filled the curved red cliffs. The rocks were as dark as pooled blood.

"Listen to the wind. Now listen again," he said. "It's a note deeper than the wind."

"What is?"

"Just listen. If you're quiet, you can hear it."

I listened to the sound of the wind in the orchard and *bosque*, and the sound of his breath. Nothing more revealed itself. Watching my face, he nodded.

"That's all right. Not everyone hears it the first time. Some don't ever hear it at all."

His expression changed, became closed off again. "Here's some practical advice. Remember to brace for the recoil.

When you fire, it's going to hit"—he jammed the butt into my shoulder—"like this."

Trying not to show he'd startled me, I clicked the safety off. "OK, I'm ready."

"See that tree? The one your old man defiled? Aim over the barrel."

"Like this?"

"Like that."

The tree was a dead *piñón* with bare branches that twisted like bonsai. I couldn't see the damage that Luke had done. Maybe the tree had magically absorbed the buckshot. Although dead, it somehow seemed to be alive—to be waiting. Even if I couldn't hear what Paul heard in the wind, I thought I understood why he loved this place—and I wondered why he'd brought us here to demolish the rightness and calm.

Arguing against keeping a gun, I'd told Luke I didn't want to call death and destruction down on my head. "You make your fate," I said. "That's ridiculous," he answered. "Like it or not, fate makes *you*. And you'd sure as hell better be ready when it does."

I closed my eyes, saw the head of the man who'd watched me. Had my voyeur intended to do more than just watch? Remembering the delicate arch of his eyebrows, I squeezed the trigger.

The shotgun slammed into me. The air broke into a million shocked particles. I felt damaged, radiant. "Did I hit it?" My voice came out in a whisper.

Paul and Luke were laughing.

"Nice try, babe," Luke said.

"You did good, Angel," said Paul. "I'm real proud, only next time you might try aiming higher, a little higher than you think you have to. You sure shot the hell out of the dirt, though. See?" He pointed at a dent in the sand twenty feet away from me. "That dirt's dead. Didn't stand a chance."

Luke had been right, you just pull the trigger. We continued my lesson for another half hour, until the sky darkened and my shoulder ached, and red shell casings gathered at my feet. Once and only once did the *piñón* tree shiver. I saw then that it wasn't alive and hadn't been for many years.

On the walk back to his house, Paul told me not to worry too much about my aim. A shotgun wasn't the most subtle firearm in the world, he said. With a weapon that punched with such a wide fist, I'd be bound to hit something. Besides, all I had to do was slow my attacker down, so I could run to safety.

Luke walked ahead of us, into the tangled gloom of the orchard. For a moment his back was a floating ghost, then he disappeared. All around the path Paul and I were on, dry grass glowed like shocks of blond hair. The air had grown cooler. The sky was a dark, clear blue, like water in a bottomless lake. Looking up made me feel dizzy, as if I was falling into the air.

Paul was saying I could keep the shotgun for as long as I wanted. "Consider it a permanent loan. You earned it, Angel."

I found myself beginning to like and even trust him. Up until now, he had only made me feel wary. At best, he provoked a vague, uneasy desire. When I'd asked Luke why be friends with such a person, he had fallen silent, then said, "He's a good man. Straight with you, there for you, good with his hands. He's a better man than you'll ever know."

"Thanks," I said to Paul. "I appreciate it."

"*No te preocupe*. You're doing me a favor." Lowering his voice, he began to tell me how his wife had never liked his firepower. Instinctively, I squinted through the darkness to make sure Luke was out of earshot. Paul and I seemed on the verge of intimacy, but I had another reason to be cautious: Luke had warned me never to utter the word "wife" in Paul's presence. He'd refused to explain why. "Can't you see the man's suffering?" "No, I can't," I'd said. "Then take it on faith," he'd told me.

All hint of a leer had gone out of Paul's voice, as if without Luke as our witness such contrivances were unnecessary. Glancing at his shadowed face, I felt moved. I wondered if he would ever sleep with me, or if loyalty would get in the way.

He was telling me that his wife's personal anti-gun lobby had been a fierce one. After the baby was born, she'd laid down the law, ordered him to get rid of his entire arsenal.

"I kept two or three old favorites hidden in the shed, though. This one's the first shotgun I ever owned. Contraband," he said. "Funny thing is, after she left I didn't care anymore. And I haven't cared. Not till you came along."

Eyes on the path, I walked more slowly. "Don't get me wrong," he murmured. "I just like the idea of you having it. I hope you never have to use it, OK?"

"OK."

I wasn't sure what I had agreed to, but Paul reached over, squeezed my hand, and released it, as if we'd just entered into a solemn pact.

Paul touched a match to the wick, and the kitchen was filled with wavering yellow light. "Make yourselves at home," he said.

The moment I stepped through the doorway, I was struck by how abandoned the house seemed. No outward sign explained the feeling. The kitchen was clean and orderly. The oil lamp glowed. There was a woodstove with a blue enamel kettle on it, and an old-fashioned ice-box, the kind that keeps the cold with blocks of ice.

We sat around the table drinking beer. I was hungry, but neither man seemed interested in food. Half listen-ing to them talk, I stared out the window at the Porvenir Valley. The near-full moon rose above the cottonwoods, slowly breaking free of the branches, as if it had got caught in the leaves. And I didn't know if it was the heat, my hunger, or the beer, but everything grew dreamy, unreal. Luke uncapped another bottle and lifted it to his mouth. The moment lasted forever. It felt as if the force that held us in time, the way gravity held us to the ground, had completely dissolved.

They were talking about a construction job in Llano Quemado. Only it wasn't construction, exactly: when they'd showed up the first day, they'd found that the work before them was demolition. The job was to tear down a house. The problem was that it wasn't just any house. The first rooms had been built in the middle of the nineteenth century, and the family that had lived in it generation after generation added on wing after wing. The work paid more than either of them was used to getting, but something wasn't right. There was history in that house. It was so well built, a work of art. Like a fortress, Luke said. A castle.

"It's a sin," Paul said.

"You see those *vigas* in the parlor, *ese?*" Luke curved his hands as if he was holding an invisible globe. "This wide. Hand hewn, too. Can you imagine that poor fucker a hundred years ago, going at it with his adze?"

They spoke as if they didn't see me, although I knew that some of their passion, the urgency of their loss, was because I was there. Kneeling, I pried the lid off the cooler and fished a hand through the icy water. My skin tingled. I wanted to say something, to enter into the easy flow of their conversation, but didn't know how. I wasn't used to drinking so much. Counting, I figured that I'd drunk four or five beers since the evening began.

"The family," I finally said. "Why did they leave?"

The talking stopped. Glancing at Paul, who was sitting very still, Luke said, "What family?"

"The one in the house. The house you're tearing down."

"Who knows? And why do you suddenly care?"

His face was sullen. For one shining second, I hated him.

"What did I do wrong now?"

"It's OK," Paul said. He looked down at the cooler, where I still knelt, and got up from his chair. "We out of fuel? There's another case in the shed."

"I'll get it."

"No, bro, you stay here."

After the door closed and we were alone, Luke tried to catch my eye, but I looked away.

"Tess, I didn't mean to sound hard, but even casual talk about families leaving cuts too close to the bone. I was only looking out for my brother."

"I don't know what you're talking about."

"Just be nice to him, that's all. He needs a little kindness right now."

When I didn't answer, he touched my shoulder. "Are you with me, Angel?"

I felt the shock of worlds colliding. "Don't call me that," I said.

"Why not?"

"Just don't."

"I see." Luke walked over to the window. The only things visible within its dark frame were the moon and the bristling trees.

"You're making a mistake if you think you're anything special," he said quietly. "You're only here because he's doing me a favor, though fuck me if I remember why I asked."

The door swung open, banging against the wall. Paul stood there with a cardboard carton in his arms. The cat ran in behind him and dashed deep into the unlit house.

"No food here, Asshole. Go kill your own." Paul narrowed his eyes. I thought I saw him smile. Setting the box on the table, he pulled three cans from their plastic cuffs.

"What's wrong, children? Are we having a quarrel?" He spoke lightly, to Luke, not me. The same complicit look had passed between the two men when the shotgun surprised me with its weight.

"No, bro. Everything's wonderful."

Luke clicked back the top of his can, and beer overflowed onto the tabletop. Paul opened his, and when it, too, overflowed, he lifted it high and let the foam stream down into his mouth. The lamplight pitted their faces with shadows. Watching them, I felt a stab of aversion for these two men who kept me around so they could feel a little more alive. I pictured myself getting up, leaving the table, and walking back to my side of the village. Maybe I wouldn't stop, I'd keep going till I reached Santa Fe or

Albuquerque. I wouldn't stop there either, I'd keep on for two thousand miles till I was back East, safe at home.

"Angel's sad," Paul was saying. "*Cabrón*, I think you ought to kiss and make up. Bury that hatchet. Come on, kiss."

Mock ceremoniously, Luke took my hand, leaned down, and kissed it.

"That's right." Paul pushed a can of beer toward me. "We've been neglecting you. You do that to angels, they fly away."

I opened my beer, watched the froth rise.

"Tell us a story," Paul said. "How did you two meet?"

They looked at me, waiting.

"At Saints and Sinners," I said at last.

"It's true," Luke said. "She was sitting at the bar all by herself, drinking a cup of coffee. At first I thought she was from here because of that long dark hair and that skin of hers. But then she opened her mouth, and it was all over. The illusion, I mean."

"What did she say?"

"That I could go fuck myself."

"Sounds like our Angel."

"So I said, 'Give me half a chance, then if you still want me to, I will. Cross my heart, hope to die.'"

"Love at first sight," Paul said.

The warm beer burned at the back of my throat. All the objects in the room—the oil lamp, the woodstove, the shotgun in the corner—seemed faraway. Paul's and Luke's voices had grown distant, too, as if they were sitting in a glass chamber apart from me. The night I'd met Luke, I had gone to Saints with Efraim, Jim, and Judy, the three other reporters at the *Sun*, to celebrate another week, another deadline met and gone. But after they'd left, I'd stayed on. I didn't want to go back to my empty house at the river's edge and was putting the moment off for as long as possible. After a week of being consumed by other people's stories, I myself was an empty house. I was afraid of what I'd find—or not find—if I wandered through the darkened rooms.

From the beginning I'd loved Luke's energy and nerve, his wiry arms, and his accented voice that proclaimed he was his own creation. He seemed utterly free, capable of anything. I thought he might even be the one who could startle me into knowing who I was, and so I was surprised that night when he took me back to the solid home he'd built on a rise above the floodplain. His voice, promising how I wouldn't be sorry, seemed to announce that he was married to this place forever. When he made love to me, urgently, almost reverently, with a tender regard for my pleasure, I'd felt a slight sting of disappointment. He was familiar after all.

"What are you, anyway? I mean, what *are* you?" Paul was saying.

His question made me alert again. "Didn't he tell you?" I listened to the hollow sound of my own voice recite that I was half Chinese and half Anglo, an explanation that explained nothing.

"Nice," Paul said. "I knew you were something, I just wasn't sure what."

Luke emptied his beer can. "Know what they call people who are half and half? Half Spanish, half Anglo, that is. *Coyote*."

"*Coyote?*"

"The same."

"Here's an interesting fact about *coyotes*. The animals, I mean," Paul said. "When they're watching you, they'll always keep just beyond firing range. Not a step farther."

"That so?" Luke said.

"You know, *cabrón*, I think I see the error of your ways. She *could* be from here."

"I told you."

"Here or anywhere."

"But she's here now. Come to papa." Luke patted his thigh. The cat, who had ventured back into the kitchen, circled his chair and gazed longingly upward. "Not you, Asshole. Her."

One, two steps, and I was on his lap. With his arms around me, I felt safe, almost accepted into Luke and Paul's small, tribeless clan. If I was a *coyote*, they were as good as *coyotes* themselves. I still don't know if that's why I asked Paul the question I asked next. I could claim I really wanted to know. I could claim, too, I believed his confession on the walk back to the house gave me the right. I could even claim I was trying to reach out, be a friend. If I said I was drunk and not thinking, that might be the truest answer, although not true enough. If I'm going to be honest, I have to admit that when I looked into Paul's glinting blue eyes, I spoke because I wanted to see how they would change.

"Where was she from, your wife?" I asked.

Paul blinked. For a moment, he seemed ordinary, like anyone else.

"That's history," he said.

"Ancient history," said Luke.

"So ancient I have no idea where she is or where my baby is either. She told me I could keep the house, she never wanted any part of it. That was the problem, she never really wanted any part of this life. She was only playing make-believe."

Paul stared at me. Luke squeezed my waist, a signal, a
warning. "I'm sorry," I murmured.

"You sure about that?" Paul said. He crushed the beer
can in his fist. The cat looked up hopefully. Suddenly
twisting, Paul hurled the can at it. It darted away, an
orange flash.

My heart beat hard, as if I'd witnessed a terrible act
of violence.

"Missed," Luke said.

"True," said Paul. "You can never hit a cat. Could get
him with a shotgun, though. Blow his little head off." He
called into the house, after the animal, "You'd run away
from home, too, if you were smart enough to figure out
how."

He pulled another beer from the six-pack and set it on
the table with a click. "You're pretty smart, aren't you,
Angel?"

"Bro," Luke said.

"No, let me finish. I've been watching you," he said to
me. "I bet you know how to run."

"Bro," Luke said again.

"One more thing," Paul said. "What kind of girl goes
to Saints alone, except to find someone like my buddy to
fuck? You got what you were after, you always do. And
when you're good and ready, you'll go back to Connecticut
or Massachusetts, or wherever the fuck you're from, just
like her."

My cheeks were hot. I tried to stare him down, but
couldn't.

"Speechless? It figures. You're not serious, *mi coyote
chinita*. You're not serious at all."

Shifting his gaze to Luke, he raked his nails up the

inside of his arm. "Watch out, brother, she'll suck you dry."

Like magic, welts rose on Paul's arm. Beads of blood welled to the surface. We all watched as one, two of the beads broke free and slid toward his wrist.

"That's enough," Luke said softly.

No one spoke. The silence felt as dense and actual as the table we sat around.

Finally Luke said, "Food. We need food." He nudged me off his lap. A few moments later he was out splitting wood while I cautiously searched the kitchen for anything edible. While we worked, Paul sat at the table with his head cradled in his arms. The empty icebox gave up a sour smell, but the shelves were lined with gleaming Mason jars filled with grains, flour, and seeds. Luke discovered a couple of onions and a carrot, and some potatoes with reddish leaves growing from the eyes. Soon we had a casserole assembled, sprinkled with herbs I'd found in canisters labeled in a clear, graceful script.

"Supper's on," Luke said.

Paul lifted his head. His face was creased from his sleeve. "You're a miracle worker, *cabrón*," he said.

After we finished eating, I curled in the big blue chair by the woodstove. The cat rasped the remains of our dinner from the plates and pans, then jumped up with me, purring.

Miraculously, Paul and Luke were talking about work again, as if blood had never been drawn. Closing my eyes, I thought of Paul's new name for me, *coyote chinita*. I knew all too well that *chinita* meant China doll, little China girl: a diminutive, an insult, an endearment. I wondered how Paul could call me something so fragile and inconsequential, and in the same breath call me *coyote*, that wild animal, that trickster. Drowsing, I wondered about the woman who'd lived here. What was her name? Had she been beautiful? What had gone through her mind while she sat in this kitchen, in this very chair, so close to the man she knew she would leave?

I must have fallen asleep because someone was gently shaking me awake.

"So it's settled. You'll sleep here, my friends." Paul's brilliant eyes swam into view. "The night is dark and the road is long, and Angel's had a hard day."

When I woke again, my mouth was filled with sand. I coughed. The room spun, not all the way around, but in short, dizzying arcs. Luke lay on the mattress beside me, sound asleep. My arms ached as if I had clawed my way up a mountain, then I remembered. I remembered everything.

It was sometime before dawn. Enough light came in through the window to illuminate the green stars some-one had stuck to the ceiling. Although the room was still spinning, I could make out a few constellations: the Big Dipper, Orion, Cassiopeia, the ones everyone knew. Against the wall opposite the bed stood a child's crib. The wood was polished to such a high sheen that even in the dim light it glowed.

I pulled on Luke's T-shirt and went into the kitchen. The room reeked of onions and stale beer, but the water that poured from the pump in the sink tasted like cool stones.

The cat wove around my legs, purring as if it was in love. When I opened the door, though, it dashed outside. Seeing the shotgun, I picked it up, careful to touch the safety, as Paul had taught me.

Outside, the real stars were so distant they sizzled with loneliness. Walking back from the outhouse, shotgun in my arms, I paused. Dogs or coyotes howled, their voices thin and luminous. I could hear the invisible river rushing below. The whole world was underwater blue. The door to Paul's house, painted deep turquoise, the Virgin's color, to ward off evil, looked like the mouth of a cave.

Instead of going back in, I found the path that led to the circle of rocks where we'd had my shooting lesson. In the orchard, small, hard apples that had fallen before they were ripe pressed through the soles of my sneakers. The ground rose, grew barren, and I was there.

I sensed his presence before I saw him. And the second I saw him, perched on a ledge near the tree I'd tried to shoot, I realized I'd been looking for him.

Paul tapped the rock at his side. "I've been waiting for you, Angel. Hop up. Don't worry, you're safe with me."

He wasn't wearing a shirt. Leaning the shotgun against the gnarled trunk, I hoisted myself next to him. That's when I saw he was completely naked. His penis was a dark blur. The pale skin that didn't get exposed to the sun looked blue, the color of blood in the veins.

He passed me the beer he was drinking. I took a sip and glanced down at his penis again, soft in its nest of blond hair. I wasn't afraid. I didn't feel desire either. His nakedness had nothing to do with me.

Taking the can back, he said, "Luke ever tell you my daughter's name? It's Ursula. When she was three, four, five months old, Ursula could cry all night long. I was proud of her will, but it drove me insane. I used to come out here just to get away."

He began to unbraid his hair. "When they left, it was

a relief, in a way. At first I dug the silence. It surrounded me. It felt like . . . like lying in a woman's arms."

His hair shimmered over his shoulders, his Amazon's chest. "I thought it was going to be all right. I even thought I'd survive. What a deluded bastard I was. The silence became my enemy, you see. Now I lie awake all night waiting for that small, willful voice that just isn't there. Like some kind of phantom limb."

At last Paul was revealing his suffering in a language I could understand. Usually, after I had coaxed a story out of a reluctant source, I felt satisfied. Now I felt disconsolate and strange.

He grew quiet again. He was listening, or seemed to be. "Hear it?" he said. "There. That hum."

I listened. The pulsing sound was almost undetectable, but then I heard it—and when I did, I wondered why I hadn't heard it before. It was everywhere, a low moan that seemed to rise from deep in the earth.

"What is it?"

"No idea."

He took my wrist and pulled me toward him, so at first I thought he wanted me after all. Instead, he squeezed my hand, so hard I could feel the bones in his fingers. The rings I wore pressed into my skin. Feeling me pull back, he let go.

"Sorry, I didn't mean to scare you."

"You didn't."

"You know," he said, "I think my buddy brought you here to save me. But you can't. Even angels like you can't do the trick." His eyes glittered. "You're all right, *querida*. Better go now. Go back home."

Relieved, I slid down from the ledge and reached for the shotgun.

"Why don't you leave that with me, Angel?"

I heard his feet hit the ground, then he was standing in front of me. When I paused, he gripped the barrel, hands above mine. My stomach tightened with terror and love.

"You don't need it now. I do," he said.

"You said I could keep it." My voice came out childish and small.

"You'll get it back, I promise. Safety's on?" He touched the stock. "Of course it is." Leaning over, he kissed me on the lips. "Now be a good girl and let go."

I spent what was left of the night in Ursula's room, watching the false stars grow slowly brighter, then pale. I imagined waking Luke, so he could go console his friend. I imagined walking back outside, naked this time, to help erase all sense of phantom limbs and loneliness. He had been waiting for me, after all. Instead, I just lay there, listening for the inevitable blast—the blast that I knew, too, would never come. While I listened, I began to understand what Paul had meant about silence—and I began to understand how phantom pain might be the worst pain of all. Because it's attached to nothing, there can be no cure.

At last the sun rose. Luke rolled onto his back, pressed his hands over his eyes. "Sweet goddess," he groaned, "let me die now. Once and for all."

The stove in the kitchen quietly thundered. I could hear it and smell the coffee and wood smoke even before Luke opened the bedroom door.

Paul sat at the table, dressed and shaved, his wet hair dripping translucent streaks onto the clean white shirt he wore. "Blood's on the stove, children. I trust you slept well," he said.

He must have gone to Pacheco's for supplies because he cooked bacon, eggs, and tortillas for breakfast. He wouldn't let me help, which I wanted to do on the chance I might catch his eye and see if what had happened in the night was real.

The morning passed without an opportunity. Before we left, he and Luke clasped hands.

"Tomorrow, *cabrón*."

"Tomorrow."

When my turn came, Paul kissed my cheek. "As promised," he murmured. "It's in Luke's truck, on the gun rack. I've passed the torch."

While Luke backed his pickup down the narrow dirt drive, Paul stood on the hill watching us. He didn't wave or smile, and I didn't either. The cracks in the windshield caught the sun, and he was almost lost in the dance of refracted light.

I would like to say that was the last time I saw him, but the truth was Luke and I visited a couple of times more. A month or so after I left Luke, I encountered Paul at Saints and Sinners, where I'd gone with the others after we'd put the *Sun* to bed. When he passed our table, he smiled, but didn't say hello. Later that night, I saw him stare at me and not look away or change expression when I caught his eye. I didn't talk to him then, although I did later that winter when I ran into him at another bar, in Santa Fe, where I'd recently moved. With his weathered skin and frayed wool shirt, he was just another man from the country coming to town. He seemed out of his element, like an unearthed treasure that crumbles the second it's exposed to air. Or maybe it was me: I had lost the ability to recognize him, to hear the secret hum beneath the noise.

Because the words he spoke weren't charged with

meaning, I don't remember them. I only remember that when he wondered aloud if we could go back to my house, and I told him there was someone else, he accepted the answer as if he'd already known. When the time came to go, he smiled wryly and said, "So long, Angel," the only hint he'd known me in El Porvenir.

The sunlight on the windshield was blinding. "Shit," Luke muttered. "Grade your fucking road, my brother." A wheel slid into a deep rut. I twisted around to the gun rack, where my shotgun was secured, and checked the safety. It was on, and a year and a half later, when I left New Mexico, the safety remained untouched. I lied to myself that I'd return it one day, but when I moved back to New York, I left the shotgun in the closet, along with the hangers and torn sheets I could no longer use.

Luke had told me never to throw a gun away, either pass it on or break it down. But when I laid the shotgun across my knees, I didn't know how to begin, how to even imagine breaking down something so solid, seamless, and deadly.

The truck lurched, and when I looked again, the angle had changed. The glass was clear. Paul was gone. I took a last glance at the orchard's unpruned branches, the sterile wilderness we had made, and, when the road dipped, the cloudless sky.

THIS WORLD

∞

He told Diana that if Sidney called out at night, not to answer. Sidney's sense of the real, which had grown thin over the years, dissolved for good after dark. He won't know who you are, Michael said. You'll confuse him, terrify him. More harm done than good.

"Remember, no matter what he says—"

"No matter what?"

"Don't go."

Michael then kissed her, so softly Diana didn't feel the warning. Later, as she tried to sleep, she remembered what he had said. It wasn't really remembering: she heard the words again, really heard them. They came out of nowhere, with a ghostly authority, as if a wall or lamp or the air had spoken. In this way, she understood that the man she loved had instructed her to ignore his father's pain.

Ruth had put her in the room next to Sidney's. The old man's door was open. From where she and Michael stood in the hall, Diana could easily see inside. The walls were painted pure white, which in the fluorescent light seemed to be tinged blue. There were, for some reason, two single beds. The unused mattress was covered with see-through plastic, while the other, on which Sidney lay, was made up with white sheets and a thin white blanket.

Sidney was the only dark and living thing in the room. The bottom half of his body was tucked into the envelope of the bed. Without his yarmulke, the balding scalp crossed by long strands of greasy hair seemed unbearably vulnerable.

"Well, good night," Michael said.

For a year now, living together, they'd said good night in bed. But in his parents' house they were going to sleep separately—her upstairs, here, and Michael down in the living room, on the foldaway couch.

"Don't be afraid," he said.

"Why should I be afraid?" Diana whispered, not wanting Sidney, or for that matter Ruth, in the master bedroom, to hear.

"No reason." Michael smiled, and it was a smile she hadn't seen on him before: the soft, proud, covert smile of a kid caught in a lie.

"Sleep tight," he said. She kissed him. He stepped into the glare of his father's room, then closed the door.

Standing in the hallway, which seemed colder now as well as dark, Diana heard murmurs, not just Michael's voice but Sidney's. She bent down to where the keyhole would've been, if it had been that kind of door. Words floated through the hollow wood—"No, Dad, she's not"— followed by a language she only knew scraps of, Yiddish.

Maybe Michael didn't know she was listening, but Diana felt the exclusion like a raised fist. Her grandmother and great aunts had done that, turned to Cantonese whenever talk entered the territory of sex or some other disgrace. For as long as she could remember, she had tried, and failed, to understand.

⌒

The room where she was to sleep was Michael's from childhood. Someone, Ruth, had placed a small bundle of carnations in a Depression-glass vase on the trunk. Diana brushed the cool tips of the buds with one finger. For the first time, she was alone in this house, the first time besides trips to the bathroom, a chamber that had unnerved her with its potpourri seashells and fringed hand towels that looked too clean to use. The rest of the house, except for Sidney's and Michael's rooms, was filled with glass and porcelain figurines, and the needlepoint still lifes Ruth did to kill time. Everything seemed so breakable and arranged. In Michael's room she could at least breathe.

His old college books lined the shelves. There was a scarred oak desk and a tensor lamp. In dresser drawers, which she lifted slightly as she pulled so they wouldn't squeak, Diana found knitted vests and soft denim, twenty years old. The room had already been combed clean of secrets. The most revealing things were the photographs that Ruth must have hung up after he'd left home.

Only one picture of Sidney and Ruth was on the wall. Michael told her it had been taken just after they'd come to America from the relocation camp in Germany. Childless then, looking more like brother and sister than husband and wife, they sat together on a park bench, holding hands. Although a whole garden spread out around them, they huddled close, smiling. Shadows brushed their lips and eyes. They both had the blurred, fragile look of people recovering from surgery.

Michael's image dominated, of course. Because of the war, Ruth and Sidney had married late. Like Diana, Michael was an only child. Cub Scout, Indian brave. The colors were a little off, the reds not true red but darker, the way dried blood is dark. Bar mitzvah, graduation. In the pictures, Michael seemed to possess a grace he'd somehow lost. Diana couldn't tell when the change had occurred: the photos ended when he'd moved to San Francisco. On this wall, twenty-one was as old as he'd ever get.

Diana and Michael had lived together in his flat near the Mission for more than a year, but although he returned to New York every two or three months, whenever he could manage, this was the first time she'd come with him. She had understood. She hadn't told her family either, not until the fact became impossible to conceal. It wasn't sub-terfuge, exactly. She was no longer a child, and besides her parents were modern, which meant they didn't demand marriage or someone Chinese or even someone younger, closer to her own age. The only one who might have had something to say was her grandmother, who had died the year before of pneumonia and was buried in a cemetery across the Bay, not in Toisan as she'd wished. To be bur-ied in Toisan was the desire of her grandmother's heart. That's how she'd put it, "the desire of my heart." Toisan was her home, their home in Guangdong, although Diana had never seen it. Her grandmother would never know about Michael. The glimmer of relief she felt was quickly lost in a haze of grief and shame.

She switched off the lamp. In the darkness that wasn't really dark—it was an incomplete, city darkness—she listened. Sidney's door clicked shut. Michael softly walked down the stairs. Springs creaked as he unfolded the couch. One wall away from her, Ruth lay in the large blue bed that she'd shared with Sidney before he got sick. Sheets rustled as Ruth turned and turned.

From Sidney's room, silence.

ﾍﾞ

At supper earlier, Diana had tried to help set the table. She'd hoped the attempt might show she was good daughter-in-law material after all, but Ruth, a small woman alive with energy, had beat her to it and laid out the silverware and napkins with faint yellow stains.

"Nothing fancy," Ruth had said. "Just food of the home."

Baked chicken, boiled potatoes. A salad made with iceberg lettuce and thin, glassy slices of onion and cucumber. Wishbone dressing. Sour pickles. With a tiny silver fork, Michael stabbed a pickle spear out of the brine.

While they ate in the kitchen, Sidney sat in his armchair in the living-dining room. Beneath him, spreading around him like his own private island, lay a plastic drop cloth.

"Aren't you going to introduce me?" Diana asked.

"Not yet," Michael said. "He knows you're here. Let's wait awhile."

From where she sat, Diana could see the window in the wall between rooms, through which full or dirty dishes could be passed. The top of the window was edged with the hanging crystals of the chandelier. Under its brilliant stalactites sat Sidney, his face in profile. He was positioned in front of the television, which was on. It had been on since they'd arrived. The year was 1991. The day before Diana and Michael landed in New York, the Gulf War had begun.

Because they'd gotten in late—due to heightened security there was a delay in St. Louis—they had stayed the first night at a motel near JFK. Cross-legged on one of the beds, with a room-service tray between them, they'd watched the screen of the bolted-down set fill with green fire.

"I hate to say it, but for once Bush is right," Michael said.

"Are you kidding?"

"It had to be done."

They'd fought in murmurs. "You don't understand. I wouldn't expect you to understand," he said. Jets rumbled over the motel roof. Neither one looked away from the TV. It had been like watching a car accident, or someone being born.

"The world," Ruth said now. She nudged the bowl of pale salad toward Diana. "The world, it only gets worse. We have people over there in Israel, he tell you? Those few of us left, a few shreds. Nephews, nieces. Children." She looked into Diana's eyes. "I am praying they are safe."

"Well," Diana said, "let's hope it's all over soon."

She tried to slice her chicken breast without getting bread crumbs on the place mat, which was made of coiled straw. The kitchen window faced the backs of brick row houses identical to the one the Kaminskis lived in. On some terraces, Weber grills glistened like wet black mushrooms. It was a cloudy winter afternoon in Brighton Beach. Behind other windows, TVs flickered with the war.

Ruth reached behind Diana. She touched a switch, and the room filled with buzzing light.

"This is delicious," Diana said.

"It's just Perdue's, from the supermarket. Cheaper than the butcher. The cost of things"—Ruth waved one hand—"the cost could break you."

Under the table, Michael squeezed her knee, but his face remained a careful blank. Diana wasn't sure what his gesture meant, if it had anything to do with love or allegiances.

"Relax," he'd told her that morning. "My mother's a human being."

Diana felt anxious about the visit for the usual reasons, but she also was ashamed of having come from a family so lightly touched by suffering. The Wongs had their dead and tortured, too—from the Cultural Revolution, although no one talked about them—but compared to the Kaminskis' dead, her dead were nothing.

"Butcher or not, it's delicious," she said.

Ruth smiled. "Thank you, dear."

Almost involuntarily, Diana glanced at Sidney. He was rocking back and forth, and she believed it was the Alzheimer's until Michael, following her eyes, said, "He's praying."

Sidney rose and began his slow, trembling, shuffling walk.

"Do you need help?" Ruth shouted. Her voice was a shock that radiated through the tiny kitchen. More gently, she added, "Go see if he needs help, dear."

"You need help, Dad?" Michael blotted his mouth on his napkin and got up. "Dad?" Michael was smiling, calmer than Diana had ever seen him. Back home in San Francisco, whenever he talked about his father or his father's disease, his jaw tensed with anger. But here, now . . .

"You going anywhere, Dad? He's not going anywhere."

Sidney stopped so that his face was centered in the window between rooms, as if he were a portrait of himself. He smiled at Diana, and she smiled back. He kept on smiling—not stopping, the way the unafflicted did—and she saw how handsome he still was, his green eyes greener than Michael's, his jaw still strong under the stubble and flaking skin.

"He likes you," Michael said.

"He does," said Ruth.

"Listen, he's saying something. Dad?"

They all waited. *In what has become a common sight in the night sky over Baghdad* . . . the television. Michael leaned down to turn the sound low.

In the softest voice that could still be heard, Sidney had said, "There is one woman, two are needed."

"What, Dad?"

"There is one woman, two are needed."

The utterance seemed to drain him. Sidney tried to turn, but couldn't get his feet around. "OK, Dad, let's go." Embracing him, Michael had helped his father back to his chair.

And now, alone in Michael's room, Diana puzzled over what Sidney had meant. The simplest answer was that Ruth was one woman, the one woman in the small, tight knot of this family. Another was needed. Her, Diana? That was too easy. What if Diana herself were one woman? In the darkness, she blushed. One woman, two. She rolled over, and the stiff sheets scratched at her. Still too literal, and besides it didn't make any sense. Maybe he meant another kind of doubling. In Chinese, two was lucky, two pomegranates on a golden chain, which her grandmother had worn on a pendant down inside her flowered dress. Two of a thing showed intent, an escape from chaos. Her grandmother tapped her chest, clicking a fingernail against the hidden metal fruit. "Luck," she'd say, as if presenting a proof. "You see?"

It was poetry. "Your father was speaking in poetry," Diana had whispered to Michael, as they'd stood in the hallway between rooms. "Everything becomes a riddle. My grandmother was like that, too."

"I don't know about poetry." Absently, Michael kissed

her. "He hallucinates, sees things. He's in another world. Remember," he told her, "no matter what he says—"

"No matter what?"

"Don't go."

Diana lay waiting for sleep. She almost got there, caught in the wind tunnel, falling fast, but at the last second she clutched the sides of the bed and opened her eyes.

Pale light from the alley filtered through the blinds. Everything in the room seemed to be made from the same gray clay. What Michael said came back to her. She heard the words, really heard them.

Cruel instructions. How necessary was this prohibition? In some essential way, Sidney had recognized her. He knew who she was. A siren whined in the distance. Diana thought she now understood the buried message in Michael's warning. He was keeping her apart from his family. If she asked, he would say he was protecting her from unpleasantness. But protection was a poor excuse. His father's illness could show her nothing she hadn't already seen with her grandmother—the oxygen tanks and bedpans, the odors, confessions, and rages. No, Michael wanted to keep her away. She could visit his home in Brooklyn, that much was allowed. She could eat chicken and pickles, sleep in his bed, talk to his mother. She could live with him, but not forever. She didn't know when the moment of separation would come, but it would. That much was clear.

Diana opened her door. Light curved up the stairway. She took it for a sign. But when she reached the living room, Michael was asleep in a snarl of blankets and sheets. The television was on, with the sound turned low.

In the changing light, he looked only half formed, not thirty-eight, not even eighteen. He didn't look like some-one who'd leave her, or someone she'd want to leave.

She slid into bed behind him. Like a boy, he was wear-ing his undershirt and Jockey shorts. He flinched, batted at her searching hands.

"What?" he muttered. "What happened?"

"It's only me."

"I thought you were someone else."

She touched his chest. His heart under her palm beat fast, as if he'd been running.

"Maybe you were dreaming," she said.

"Maybe. Maybe I still am."

He pushed her fingers lower, under the elastic, to where he was hard, and she felt the pang that sometimes came when he was aroused while asleep or just on wak-ing: evidence of a desire that had nothing to do with her.

"Now?" she said. "Are you sure?"

His hand continued to guide hers. "We have to be quiet," he murmured.

She turned away from him, so they could arrange their bodies the way they liked it when they were tired, her back pressed against his stomach. But when they moved, the bed exploded in a squeal of springs. Trying to choke back laughter, Michael bit into the T-shirt she'd worn for a nightgown. His mouth left a cool wetness between her shoulder blades.

"Come on," Diana whispered. She was laughing, too, soundlessly, unable to stop. "Down here." They lay on the Persian rug in front of the TV, at the edge of Sidney's plastic island, Michael beneath her, holding her hips. While they made love she found herself, almost against her will, glancing up at the screen, at the reporter in a flak jacket who stood talking on a roof somewhere under a desert sky.

Suddenly, almost violently, Michael pushed her off of him. Diana hadn't used her diaphragm and was grateful, she thought, that he'd managed in time. She hadn't come, but she was used to not coming.

"Oh, you seductress." Michael kissed her ear. "Why do you always get your way?"

She felt a sharp, slight pain, as if someone had rapped her on the ankle with a cane. Startled, Diana stood up. The front of her shirt was sticky, stained. A broken figurine of a woman in a long blue dress lay on the floor. The hook held by the tiny, severed hand was still intact. A shepherd's crook.

"Oh my God." Kneeling, Diana gathered up the pieces of the shepherdess. She must have bumped into the knickknack stand when she stretched out her legs. Her throat tightened, as if she'd injured something alive.

Upstairs, the hall light blinked on. For an instant, Michael froze. "Wonderful," he said. He struggled into his jeans, tossed Diana his sweater. They heard one door open, then another. "If we're lucky, she's just checking on him," he whispered. He stuffed his shorts under the pillow. By the time Ruth came walking slowly down the steps, her swollen legs lifting from the part in her robe, Michael and Diana were seated on the bed, breathless, staring at the set.

At the bottom of the staircase, Ruth stood staring at them. Diana couldn't see her face, just a backlit aurora of tangled hair.

"Hi, Ma."

"I can't sleep," Ruth said.

"I couldn't either," said Diana. The need to confess

swelled inside her. "I have an apology to make, I broke your blue lady."

Ruth walked unsteadily toward them.

"Yes, I thought perhaps I heard sounds."

She sank into Sidney's armchair. With a brief look of sorrow, she took in the shattered figure that Diana held in her hands.

"Don't worry, dear," she said. "What are a few pieces of clay in this world?"

Michael got up. "Want some tea, Ma? I'll make some tea."

"That would be very nice. Just dip the bag once, maybe two times."

Kitchen cabinets creaked, and the microwave began its low roar. Ruth and Diana gazed straight ahead at the television, the top of which was covered with more photos of Michael. Schoolboy, pirate, a teenager with long, neat hair.

"He's quiet, thank God," Ruth said softly. "Like a baby, he's sleeping."

"Good. I mean, I'm glad."

Ruth pinched the flaps of her robe together. Green light streaked the televised sky. "He was a great mind once," she said. "You wouldn't know it now. All day long, reading. If we had stayed in the village we were from"— she glanced at Diana—"the village in Poland, he would have been a scholar."

"Did you know him then?"

"Of course I knew him. Everybody knew everybody. Only, later . . ." Ruth paused. "Later, at the camp, the relocation camp, when we met again . . . you would not believe the happiness of being alive. We were so grateful to find someone from home, you might say we married for gratitude. It is not bad, to marry for this. People marry for worse."

In the kitchen, a teaspoon clinked against glass.

"Do you ever want to go back?" Diana asked.

"Where?"

"To your village. In Poland."

Laughing, Ruth shook her head. "What is left there for us?"

They heard steps.

"He's coming," Ruth said. "Quick, tell me what is happening with this war, this terrible and necessary war."

"Nothing," Diana answered. "They keep replaying the same footage. A lot of talk, but nothing new I can see."

Ruth held the saucer and cup of weak tea in her lap. "You'd like some?" she asked Diana. "Dear, offer your sweetheart some tea."

"She doesn't want any."

"That's OK," Diana said. "I don't. Really, I don't."

Ruth sternly scrutinized them both. "I always wait before I drink. If it's too hot, it burns."

From time to time, Michael touched the remote, changing channels. Desert Storm was everywhere. Green light, exploding jewels. A distant fire, shadowed minarets. In the dimness, Diana fiddled with the chunks and splinters of porcelain, trying to see how they might fit together again, until Ruth said, "You're making me nervous, dear."

When Diana kissed Michael on the cheek, he gave her a suspicious look.

"I feel sleep coming on." More loudly, she said, "Good night, Ruth."

"Sleep well, dear. For what is left of this night, sleep well."

But as Diana lay between the sheets, the loneliness returned. She touched the crumpled T-shirt, rough hair, wetness. One hand began to work. With the other, she lifted the sheet and blankets away from her body, so no one would hear the rustling.

For her imagined text, she chose what she and Michael had just done, the danger of it, the threat of discovery. But when she finally came, the image she held was of Sidney's rocking body, and his mouth and eyes.

She must have fallen asleep, because the voice woke her.

"Help me. Please help me."

It was Sidney.

"Will no one help me?"

Diana's eyes fluttered open. An unremembered dream circled the room and disappeared. Dim light filled the window, but she couldn't tell if it was dawn or the street-lights' mercury glow.

"Will no one help?"

She lay in bed, listening. *English*. He was speaking English, to her. He wasn't in another world: he wasn't in any world but this.

"Please help."

She got up. The door creaked open. In the white room, which shimmered with its own bluish light, Sidney lay propped against the pillows, his hair clumped like wet weeds around his face. His eyes were impossible to read.

He was silent. Had he really spoken?

The odor of urine and shit assaulted her. Trying not to breathe, she crouched beside him.

"It's me, Diana," she said slowly. "Diana, Michael's friend. Michael, your son."

His stare shifted from her face to the hand she rested on the metal bars that kept him from falling.

"Sorry." She slid her fingers off the cool steel. "Sidney," she said, "I'm here to help. Tell me how to help you."

His eyes gleamed. Tears streaked the dry cheeks and gathered on his chin.

"Sidney, what is it? Tell me what it is."

"Please," he whispered, in a voice so soft it almost failed to exist. "Please . . ."

She wanted to let him know she knew. Trying to smile, she leaned closer. "One woman. I'm one woman."

Tears covered his face. "Please," he said, "please don't hurt me."

She hadn't heard him enter, but Michael was standing behind her. "Dad, it's OK. It's all right now, it's all right." More words followed, in Yiddish, the language they shared.

Michael removed the rail, nudged one shoulder under Sidney's limp arm, and lifted him out of bed. With the other hand, he braced his father's chest. Slowly, together, like lovers, they began to walk.

The hall light clicked on. "Go back to sleep, Ma," Michael called. "I'll take care of him. You sleep. Somebody in this house ought to get some sleep."

Diana tugged at the reeking sheets. "Leave them," he said quietly. "Just leave them alone. I told you. You know I told you."

The bathroom door swung open. Still weeping, Sidney disappeared with his son, and Diana knew, not by the words but by Michael's cold, sad smile, that it would be over soon.

A year later, long after she'd moved back to her parents' house in Berkeley, Sidney died. She and Michael hadn't spoken for months—the end had been bitter—but he called to tell her.

"I'm sorry," Diana heard herself say. "I am so sorry."

She sat in the living room. On the cherrywood cabinet in the corner was a shrine to her grandmother. It wasn't an obvious shrine, just two small bunches of dried flowers and a photograph in a standing frame. In the photo, her grandmother, wearing her black-rimmed glasses, was an unsmiling old woman. Old and ordinary. Beloved.

Sidney had died in his sleep, kissed by God, Michael said. He and Ruth sat shiva, neither bathing nor changing their clothes. People visited the house, brought food, and prayed. He said he was grateful for the ritual, for the surprising comfort it could bring.

She told him she was glad he could find comfort somewhere.

"Well, good-bye," he said.

"I *am* sorry."

"I know."

For the rest of the week, she had trouble sleeping. On that first anniversary of the war, the news channels reran Desert Storm. Much more was now known. Collateral damage had turned into hundreds of thousands of Iraqi dead. The way the anchors eulogized the whole hellish, swift business, it sounded as though the war—if it could be called a war—had played itself out in the distant past.

Long after her parents went to bed, Diana stayed up in the den, switching stations. She stared at the flashing green sky and remembered how, a year ago, she and Michael and the whole country, gripped by a helpless sense of urgency, had done nothing but watch.

Although it was cold, she sat on the floor. The Gulf War was over. On the news now was a tractor-trailer moving slowly down a snow-covered freeway. She hit the power button and the TV went dark. A faint gray light emanated from the screen. The sensation she felt wasn't grief. She wished it was; grief would have been easier. All she knew was that when the conflict ended, and she and Michael turned off the TV at last, the home they'd shared filled with a silence that was never completely broken again.

TROUBLES

ᗧᔆ

On the way to the wedding, they fought about what to name the baby.

Andrew insisted on Marian, the name they'd chosen for their first daughter. While he argued his point, Hanna stared out the passenger-side window at the mountains wrapped in curtains of rain. This was the first real storm of the season. Although it was only August, the leaves were already turning brown because of the long drought. Even the torrents pounding on the car roof now couldn't repair the damage.

"Don't," she said quietly. "Don't say another word. Please just shut up."

Andrew's eyes were wet. These days he cried often and easily, as if releasing the backlog of tears left unwept over the past two years. His neck craned unhappily forward. Out of reflex, she reached across the space between their seats to massage the tension away, but then, remembering, drew her hand back.

"I wish we could just fucking move on," he muttered.

"That's not the issue."

He didn't answer. She wanted to tell him he was wrong, she *was* moving on, but it was too late, silence had set in. She listened to the rain. The baby turned inside her, a flutter-bump of mysterious life. A month ago, Dr. Selig, who had three daughters himself, called to deliver the news that everything was all right and that the baby was a girl. "Congratulations," he said. "Your troubles are just beginning." Even so, Hanna didn't fully believe the pregnancy was real. The early weeks had passed in a dream, from which she'd only begun to awaken now that she'd reached the fifth lunar month—the month in which she had lost their first child.

"Is this the turnoff?" Andrew's voice was rich with accusation.

"Yes, here."

Somewhere behind the clouds, the full moon glowed. Virginia wanted to get married under that moon, but the weather had obliterated her hopes. She and Wei lived in the country full-time, unlike Andrew and Hanna, both writers and college professors who were spending their second summer in the cabin Virginia had found for them. For the down payment, they'd used what they had saved for the first baby so Hanna could take a semester off. They'd never talked about the terrible need to get rid of the money, just as they had never seriously talked about buying a house; but during that first empty spring, when they'd driven all over Greene County on the pretext of seeing what was out there, Hanna knew that Andrew, like her, was compelled to find a place untouched by sorrow.

The road wound higher and higher through woods broken by houses and meadows. Gradually, the tension in the car faded. Most of their fights ended this way, by simply ceasing to be. She sometimes worried about this marital habit, which grew out of laziness or love, as if all that was unresolved between them was deposited in a large room that one day might not be large enough to contain it. Love that lasted, she believed, depended on a slow but constant accretion of joy.

Mist surrounded the car. Andrew set the windshield wipers on low.

"Watch out!" Hanna cried.

The eyes of the two deer glowed red in the headlights. Andrew swerved and slowed. The legs supporting their bodies seemed impossibly thin. Their wet coats were speckled white, their startled ears delicate, thin shells.

"Fawns," she murmured.

"I hope they learn caution, or they're not long for this world."

The fawns pivoted and leapt into the woods. Their white tails flickered like flames, then disappeared. Hanna settled back into her seat. The creatures seemed to be the souls of their two children, the one they'd lost and the one still waiting to be born. Often when she had such thoughts, she told them to Andrew—the only other person who might understand. But now she kept quiet. The echo of their argument still faintly resonated, and she didn't want to reawaken the unhappy business with a single word about babies.

Through the rain and prematurely dark dusk, the canopy tent erected in Virginia and Wei's front yard glowed eerily red. When they got closer, Hanna saw that the glow emanated from the Chinese lanterns hanging from the edges. Sheets of clear plastic covered the open sides. The red-lit people who thronged within looked like ghosts of the drowned trapped in a luminous lake.

She followed Andrew through the part in the plastic curtain, closed her umbrella, and scanned the crowd. After three months away from the city, it felt strange to be among so many people. Most wore colorful, slightly wrinkled but expensive-looking clothes. The easy laughter told Hanna that many of them already knew one another.

Virginia, the bride, was the real-estate agent who'd helped them find their cabin. During the hours driving the back roads in Virginia's Rover—she spent far more time with them than their budget seemed to warrant—a friendship had formed. Hanna liked her unagentlike eccentricities—the odd barrettes she wore in her gray-streaked red hair, her openness, the outpouring of stories from her life, the trees and perennials in her garden named for dead friends and family: the red maple for Tom, the peonies for Ali, the ornamental cherry for her mother. Virginia loved classical Chinese poetry, and in her spare time translated poems from the Tang Dynasty and practiced speaking a passable Mandarin.

Hanna didn't speak Mandarin or, for that matter, Cantonese, although if the conversation remained concrete, she could follow the gist of what was being said. The farther the talk strayed from physical realities—the table, the food on the table, the health of the person she was talking to—the less she understood. She also understood less when listening to a stranger, as if her knowledge of the language was inextricably bound to parents, grandparents, cousins, aunts. The same sentence spoken by someone outside the web of family might go uncomprehended. Language wasn't supposed to work that way, though. One of its beauties, she told her students, was that the written word could bridge the void between one person's imagination and another's. While she didn't really think it was that simple, she had faith in stories and their ability to move those who actually read them.

Most of the wedding guests were standing and talking,

although a few sat at the tables swathed in white cloth.
Besides Virginia and Wei, whom they'd had dinner with
once, they knew no one.

"I'll find our seats," Andrew said.

"Hey there, Mama!" Virginia, in a sparkling yellow
dress, came up behind them. Her fingernails bright with
golden polish, she patted Hanna's belly. Like almost
everyone else—friends, family, strangers—she aimed
high, instead of more accurately below, in the private
reach between Hanna's navel and groin where the baby
invisibly squirmed.

"Hello, little work-in-progress. Got a name?"

"Not yet." Andrew kissed Virginia's cheek. "You look
great, Gin."

"Bless you for coming."

"You're the one who deserves the blessing." Smiling,
Hanna hugged her. Coming to the wedding had been a
mistake. They should have stayed home and watched the
rain, instead of venturing out where her pregnancy was on
public display. She wasn't as superstitious as her grandmother, who worried about jealous gods, but she wished
that she could wordlessly wait out the time till the baby
was born. If she held her breath, this one might make it. If
she had her choice, this child would float nameless inside
her, as protected by silence as she was by the muscle-and-
membrane-shored sea in Hanna's body.

"Sorry about your moon," she told Virginia.

"The moon's still there, you just can't see it." Glancing
searchingly across the room, Virginia said, "Forgive me,
but I seated you guys with the famous ex."

The famous ex was Wei's first wife, Naomi Breton, Nai.
Nai was an artist of some kind, although not as success-
ful as Wei. Her fame didn't arise from her art, but from

all the stories Virginia had told about her while they drove from house to prospective house. In the only story Hanna remembered, Virginia opened the front door one day, soon after still-married Wei had moved in with her and her daughters, to find a raku-glazed bowl on the mat. The bowl was so large that Virginia could have stood in it. The glaze was a crackled blue the color of the sky early in the morning. Even at first glance Virginia could see that it had been made not on the wheel but by hand, the coils of clay pressed into thin walls that still bore the fingerprints of its maker. In the bowl was a pool of clear liquid. Before she could think, Virginia leaned down and dipped her finger in. It was still warm.

"A textbook case," Virginia told Hanna and Andrew. While she went on and on about passive aggression, Hanna sat quietly in the backseat. Nai's gesture seemed perfect, and she wanted to savor that perfection instead of dissecting it.

The other thing Hanna remembered about Nai was that she and Wei had tried for years to have a child, and when she finally conceived, there had been some kind of problem. When she asked for details, Virginia glanced meaningfully at Andrew, then told her she didn't want to know.

"The justice of the peace is late," Virginia said now. "Wei's about to kill someone. I better stop him before he does."

She let Hanna kiss one powdered cheek, then was gone.

They found their seats, metal folding chairs that were cold to the touch. Hanna's seat was wet. Andrew used a wad of Kleenex to wipe it off. In the middle of the table was a vase jammed tight with orange day lilies. A small brown spider clung to the underside of one pointed petal.

"I'll get us drinks," Andrew said. He didn't want to be

there either, she knew, although his reluctance had to do with a loathing for ritual.

Amid the swirls of rayon and raw silk, Wei's family stood out in their suits and ties and tailored dresses. Style was what set them apart; their Chineseness, like Hanna's, seemed almost secondary. By Wei's family's brand of elegance and obvious wealth, she knew them to be pure upper-crust Hong Kong. Wei's mother—although she looked no older than sixty, she had to be the mother—appeared as powerful and confident as the chair of some international corporation, which, perhaps, she was.

Her eye came to rest on the woman Wei's mother was talking to—a very thin, very pale white woman in a short black dress. It wasn't just her choice of color, the only dark spot at the wedding, that caught Hanna's attention, but the nervous, angry energy that both dared and defied anyone who might want to look.

The mood in the tent intensified. People began to drift toward the tables. "Time to get in our places," said a man wearing a Hawaiian shirt with ukiyo-e cresting waves.

The woman in black wandered from table to table, squinting at the placards, which had been written in glitter and Magic Marker by Virginia's daughters. Hanna glanced at her own, lettered in blue sequins. A superfluous "h" ended her name.

Andrew came back from the bar with their drinks. "Mineral water, no ice," he said, setting the plastic cup before her.

"Did you see where the bathroom is? I have to pee."

"Excuse me, I think this is my seat," said the woman in black.

Andrew pulled the chair out for her, bumping the legs over knots of grass.

"Thanks," she said, grimacing a quick smile. "Jim!" She waved one arm so thin that the hand at the end looked unnaturally large. "Jim, over here."

Hanna hadn't expected Nai to come to the wedding with a man. In Hanna's imagination she was a woman swaddled in wounded solitude, but Jim looked normal enough, his thinning brown hair pulled back in a pony-tail, crow's feet bearing witness to careless hours spent in the sun.

He grinned at Hanna and Andrew, then sat down.

"Everyone!" the man in the Hawaiian shirt called. "Everyone, we're about to begin."

People seated near the head table, which was the rec-tangular table facing all the round ones, stood up. Wei, smiling in his white guayabera shirt, looked nothing like a man about to kill, as Virginia had described him fifteen minutes earlier.

"I guess we're supposed to stand," said Jim.

Flowers threaded through their braids, Virginia's daugh-ters walked down the path between tables. Some of the guests began to hum the wedding march. Others took up the tune. A kazoo and a flute joined in. A gust of rain lashed the tent, denting its plastic sides. Virginia appeared. She now wore a circlet of white and pink roses in her hair and was holding a bouquet. Giggling, she wove her way through the tables.

Throughout the brief ceremony led by the man in the Hawaiian shirt, Hanna kept stealing glances at Nai, who leaned slightly forward, as if straining to hear every word. Hanna thought about the beautiful ash-fired bowl filled with urine. Why had Nai come to watch the man who once was her husband marry the woman he'd left her for? Among the tanned wedding guests, she looked as wary

as a pale-dark animal that had blundered from the forest
onto the shoulder of a busy road.

Nai's hand was wrapped around a plastic cup of red
wine. When the vows were said, she took a sip. Wei leaned
down and, holding Virginia's face between his hands,
kissed her. Everyone applauded and cheered. Politely,
it seemed, Nai made clapping motions. Instead of palm
meeting palm, though, she soundlessly tapped the outside
of her cup. What still bound her to Wei? They couldn't
be counted among the ex-couples who'd become friends.
They didn't have children. Then Hanna remembered—
how could she have forgotten?—the lost child.

Turning to Nai with a sudden surge of warmth, she
held out her hand and said, "I'm Hanna."

Nai's hand was cool to the touch. She took Hanna in
and, as if for the first time, glanced at her belly in the too-
tight green dress.

"How far along are you?" She was smiling, but her
smile was forced, and Hanna remembered—a memory
already wrapped in the gauze of forgetfulness—how just
a few months ago the sight of a pregnant woman could
bring her to tears.

The ceremony was over. Most of the guests were gathered in a circle, at the center of which stood Virginia and
Wei.

Nai sat down, so Hanna did, too.

"Five months." Hanna smiled apologetically. "I'm sorry.
I mean, I heard about your loss. I lost one, too."

Nai gazed at her with new interest, Hanna thought.
"How?" she asked.

Hanna had told the story many times before. In the
first weeks, the telling had been gilded with the passion
of new grief. As weeks became months, and the months

multiplied, she told it because she needed to understand, to make sense of a loss so large, so fraught with complexity that it eclipsed everything else her life had been till then. Later she told the story more quietly to find solace in other women who'd made the same decision. Once she started looking, she'd found so many of them, so terribly many, and together they formed a secret tribe—secret because what they'd done was almost taboo, secret because almost no one else understood their agony. After all, hadn't it been their choice?

Often when she told the story, she saw and felt what she described. She saw the karyotype that spelled out her baby's flawed genetic destiny, black snakes and dots and Xs on a white field. She saw the operating room, the masked attendants, the brilliant light above. It was cold, why was it so cold? Dr. Selig wore plastic goggles because, oh God, it was going to be messy. "You're thinking too much. Stop," he told her. Raising his goggles, he smiled sadly, sympathetically. Then he lowered the oxygen mask over her face, and the sound of her own breathing was all she heard.

Hanna hadn't told the story to anyone since becoming pregnant again. Although she didn't believe in her grandmother's jealous gods, she didn't want to jinx the new baby. But she told it now because ever since the day Virginia said, "You don't want to know," she'd understood that she and the famous ex had something in common. They shared the same anguish. An anguish so deep, Hanna told her now, that she couldn't bear to let the baby's remains be incinerated as medical waste. They found a funeral home that agreed to handle the cremation. Andrew wanted to dispose of the ashes right away, but she couldn't let go. Thirteen months after the abortion, they finally did scatter them in the East River, under the Brooklyn Bridge. What she didn't tell Nai was that in the month that followed, she conceived again.

Nai's wide hazel eyes were fixed on her. Hanna knew the words by heart, but for some reason the story was difficult to tell—not because the telling reawakened the pain, but because this time it didn't. Her voice sounded hollow, as if someone else was talking. Although everything she said was true, it felt like a lie.

Finally, she was done. By now most women would have reached across the table to touch her hand. At the very least their faces would soften with sorrow, hers and their own, and this was the best part, the connection, the sense that she wasn't the only inhabitant of the awful world made by pain.

But Nai only stared. Her attitude was unapologetic, her face the face of a woman who didn't have to pretend.

"And you? What happened to yours?" Hanna said.

Nai blinked. "Two," she said softly. "I had two."

Instinctively, Hanna cupped her hand protectively over her belly. She was vaguely aware that another couple was standing by the empty seats across the table. Andrew and Jim half rose to shake hands, but she couldn't move.

Pleasantries were exchanged. Almost against her will, she heard the man announce that while they were up here in the Catskills, he was going to get a little fly-fishing in.

"Why do they whip the rod back and forth like that?" Andrew asked.

He had no interest in fly-fishing, but was acting as if. If you act as if, he'd told Hanna, they keep talking so you don't have to.

"When I finally got pregnant the first time, I didn't want to do the amnio," Nai was saying. "I wanted the baby, or thought I did. No matter what."

"But?"

"But. My husband."

"Wei?"

"He can't handle uncertainty. I mean, look at his paint-ings. He's good, but he could be better. He's a strict real-ist—not because it's *him*, but because he's afraid of where his imagination might take him."

The brown spider on the centerpiece now hung in the air below its orange petal. Following Hanna's eyes, Nai held out one finger and touched the invisible thread. They both watched the creature curl and fall.

"An anomaly," Nai said. "That's how they described it. Something called translocation."

A tiny piece of one chromosome had broken off and attached itself to another. Nai's doctor and the geneticists had never seen that configuration before, and because they'd never seen it, they couldn't say what it meant.

"The baby might have been retarded or deformed, or it might have been normal. There was no way of knowing."

She leaned down for her purse, fumbled, found a pack of cigarettes. She shook one out—a filterless, Hanna saw—but stopped short before lighting it.

"Sorry," she said. "I almost forgot. You're probably not into secondhand smoke."

Nai's thorny anger was gone. Her face looked blurred, the way a child's does the moment before it realizes it's about to cry. Music began to play, a zydeco band. Hanna thought about reaching out to touch the thin bare arm, but didn't know how. After all, they were still strangers.

"You want something so much. And then," she said. "And then."

"I know," Hanna said. But she was no longer sure.

A girl with hennaed hair set salad plates before them.

Smiling her thanks, Hanna tried to suppress her growing uneasiness, the sense that Nai was somehow cursed. That it was bad luck to sit so close.

"Wei and I were already on shaky ground. I knew I couldn't raise an impaired child alone." Nai gave an unhappy laugh. "Not when I'm an impaired child myself."

She stared down at her plate and Hanna stared, too, at the white square of feta cheese atop the mound of greens. Nai seemed detached, spent, like someone who'd just confessed and was done talking, but Hanna had to know.

"The second one? What happened to the second one?"

Nai startled out of her dream. "Oh that," she said. "The second time, I had the amnio done early. At twelve weeks, before I could feel the baby move."

"And?"

"Down syndrome. Just like yours." She tapped the cigarette against her thumbnail, then let it drop. "It was easy. Easier. A piece of fucking cake."

Nai stood up. Her leg struck the edge of the table, hard. "Shit," she muttered.

Everyone around the table stopped talking, as if glad for the excuse.

"Going somewhere, babe?" Jim asked.

"Nowhere," she muttered. "Nowhere at all."

"Wait," Hanna said, but Nai was already shouldering her way through the crowd.

When Hanna rose, Andrew looked up at her questioningly. Seeing the answer in her eyes, he nodded.

Following Nai's trail, she passed Virginia and Wei, who stood between tables packed with relatives and friends. Wei said something, and everyone laughed. For a second,

Wei's mother eyed Hanna, sizing her up. Hanna knew, because it had happened so many times before, that Wei's mother would deign to talk to her only if the situation demanded, and if it came to that, in English alone. She now saw that they—she and Andrew, Nai and Jim, the fly-fishing couple—had been deliberately placed at the outer edge of the party. The bores, the ex-wife, the clients. The women who lost the children they'd never had.

Nai parted the curtain and ran into the darkness. Hanna took a breath, then followed. The rain pelted down, plastering her hair to her face, slicking her dress to her body. For a moment she thought Nai was going to dart into the forest, dooming her to follow. Then the door to the house swung open, carving a path of light into the grass. Framed in the doorway, Nai paused. Drenched, she looked even thinner, like a little girl. The door closed. The path of light was gone. Virginia's garden, with its flowers named for the dead, spread invisibly around Hanna. She stood on the grass in the cold rain.

She was afraid that Nai had locked the door, but it opened easily. Water spread around her feet onto the wide slats of the floor. She saw that she was standing in what years ago had been the kitchen. The fireplace was deep and blackened, like a small cave. In it sat a copper cauldron filled with bundles of dried blue flowers, which Hanna understood to be purely decorative, as were the bunches of herbs that hung upside down from the low beams. Everything here, useful in a past age, was meant to be beautiful, and beautiful alone.

On the wall hung three small paintings by Wei: day lilies, a green pear sliced in half, and a nude, a red-haired woman with a lush Renaissance body modeled, no doubt, after Virginia. *A strict realist.* She leaned forward to study the nude, then stopped and looked around, but there was still no sign of Nai. It was as if the house had swallowed her.

Beneath the paintings sat a large blue bowl. Was it the same bowl Nai had left on the doorstep? It was now filled with pink and pale orange seashells, the kind that looked like rose petals made of bone. Walking down the narrow hallway, Hanna thought of the burning that had made it beautiful. *A piece of fucking cake.* The feelings Nai inspired were too dangerous to examine closely, but she knew that anger was part of the mix, along with pity and awe. She also felt guilty because something had gone wrong in the telling of stories. Instead of finding each other, she and Nai had been driven apart, and she, Hanna, was to blame.

Upstairs, she opened the door to Wei and Virginia's room. "Are you there?" she called. The door to a daughter's room stood open. "Nai?"

Behind the last door was a trundle bed so small it had to belong to the youngest daughter. Hanna took off her sandals, lay down, and pulled the flowered quilt over herself. The sheets smelled like fallen leaves. Curled on her side, she felt the baby move, a flicker of tiny, unseen limbs. "Little one," she murmured.

The floorboards creaked. Hanna startled awake. She became aware of her body again: the muscled drum of her belly, her wet clothes, hunger, and need to urinate. She had slept, she knew, longer than she should have.

She heard laughter. Women's voices.

"What a relic," the first voice said. "I wonder where Virginia found her."

"If she said another word about how good the food

was . . ." The second woman started to laugh, the full laugh of a woman unafraid of how she sounded.

Hanna wandered back into Wei and Virginia's room. One woman was seated on the bed, the other on the love seat next to the dressing table. They both looked to be Wei's age, in their early fifties, and were beautiful in an unfussy manner that had little to do with men. Hanna found herself instantly drawn to them.

The one in the red sarong widened her eyes when she saw Hanna.

"Don't move an inch."

She went out into the hall, returning a moment later with a purple bath towel, which she draped around Hanna's shoulders like a mantle.

"You don't want to catch your death," she said.

"When are you due?" asked the other woman, whose long, loosely bound hair was entirely silver.

"January," said Hanna.

"A millennial baby."

"Completely unplanned. I mean planned, but not that way."

They laughed, and Hanna joined in. The two women radiated a sense of calm mirth. They seemed as lucky as Nai was unlucky. The arms, neck, and bosom of the woman in the red sarong were freckled and soft. She was comfortable inside her skin, and Hanna knew, without knowing how, that the woman and her friend were both mothers.

"May I?"

Hanna nodded. The woman in red rubbed her pregnant dome at the navel, the sure and knowing touch of someone who has borne a child herself.

"Are you a painter?" Hanna asked, because it seemed the only possible thing she could be.

"Yes. Yes and no. I have five of these, five bambinos. The youngest's eighteen this year." Lifting her hand away, she said, "Know if it's a boy or girl?"

"A girl."

The woman glanced at her friend, and they exchanged approving smiles.

"It's nice when your first is a girl," she said. "This *is* your first?"

Hanna thought of the two fawns, their delicate, breakable-looking bones.

"No," she said. "I lost one."

The woman's eyes brimmed. Like footprints in wet earth, they filled but didn't overflow. Suddenly, her arms were around Hanna. Stunned by the outbreak of feeling, she breathed in the scent of warm flesh and wine.

"I lost my first, too."

She pulled away from Hanna, then spread her hands the width of a sheet of paper. "He weighed a pound and a half when he was born. A pound and a half, can you imagine? So light he almost wasn't there."

"Joyce, honey," the silver-haired woman said.

"No, I'm fine." She took a step back, but didn't wipe her eyes. Smiling, she said, "You enjoy that baby. They don't stay babies for long."

In the bathroom after she washed her hands, Hanna unbuttoned her damp dress and stared at the mirror.

The image on the door surprised her. They didn't have a full-length mirror in the cabin, and this was the first time in almost three months she'd seen her entire pregnant self reflected back to her. She'd known the nipples had grown large and chocolate dark, but hadn't noticed the veins that glowed beneath the skin. The dark line that divided the curve of her belly looked as definite as if someone had drawn it with an eyebrow pencil.

But the most amazing thing was how round she'd grown, as if she'd changed into someone else. A mother. Joyce had been thus transformed at least six times. She and Nai, poor Nai, twice.

Two years ago she'd been so consumed by grief that she couldn't imagine living. Mourning and waiting, the double sorrow of loss and waiting to conceive again, had worn her and Andrew down to the bone.

Now she was the woman in the mirror. Slowly, she buttoned up her dress.

Outside, it was still raining, but more gently now. She held the purple towel over her head, felt the cool drops slide down one wrist. Behind the thinning cloud cover, the moon shone, touching the trees and the meadow beyond with its quiet light. She walked through Virginia's garden, pausing to better feel the magic of Joyce's blessing. Globed hydrangeas, storm-flattened leaves. Bars of scented soap hung from the posts to ward off deer. Heavy with rain, star lilies drooped to the ground. The first time she'd toured the garden, she had been slightly shocked by the ease with which Virginia named the dead. "This is my dear friend Gina," Virginia had said, running a finger over the red-tipped petals of a Peace rose.

When she finally agreed with Andrew it was time to dispose of the baby's ashes, he suggested they plant a tree on their land and bury them at the roots. Some kind of flowering tree, he said, like a dogwood or peach. The idea sounded good at first, but what if the tree failed to thrive? What if it died before she did, and in its death she'd have to endure that other death again? Worse, what if they sold the land, moved away? How could she bear to leave it behind?

She had to be certain. The only certainty lay in letting go, so one raw Sunday early in spring, they went down to the landing below the Brooklyn Bridge and tossed the ashes into the river. The water looked as densely taut as mercury. For a second, Hanna thought the ashes would float on its silvery surface out to sea, but what remained of their first child's body pierced the surface and sank into the blackness below. How little of her there really was. Two, three handfuls of fine gravel. Some of the bone chips had burned to shell-like shades of pink and blue. She had traveled from one ocean through the fire into another without ever having to endure dry life.

Hanna had failed to explain all this to Nai. She'd talked about her last unborn daughter as if she were still deep in sorrow, but the truth was she'd begun to outlive sorrow. *Marian.* She and Andrew loved the sound of the name, had loved it and said it aloud to each other so many times that when one of them finally looked it up in *20,000 Baby Names*, it almost didn't matter that Marian meant "bitterness."

The zydeco band was playing a fast song. At the far corner of the dance floor Hanna saw a flash of black, Nai dancing with Jim. His hand cupped one jutting shoulder blade. She was beautiful, Hanna realized. Why hadn't she noticed before?

Jim said something, and Nai nodded. Then they dipped and turned so that Nai was facing her, but either she didn't see Hanna or pretended not to. There was no sign of recognition in her face.

Hanna folded the purple towel, then laid it over the back of a vacant chair. The dreamlike urgency she'd felt running after Nai was gone. What would she have done if she'd found her? What could she say? How could she apologize for the sin of pretending they walked the same road?

Andrew sat alone, writing something in the notepad he always carried. She felt a rush of love so strong her throat ached.

"The waitress really wanted to clear the table," he said after she sat down. "You should have seen me battle to save your plate."

He recapped his pen and put it in his shirt pocket. The vein in his temple pulsed. "You missed the cutting of the cake. Just the kind of ritual you enjoy. What took you so long? I was getting worried."

She thought about how the story would sound and knew even before the words formed that she couldn't tell it.

"I went after Nai."

"I know. A fellow traveler?"

"Yes."

Andrew lifted the napkin tented over her plate. Chicken and new potatoes. She breathed in the scent of rosemary, thyme. "Thank you, love."

"I saved some cake, too. Carrot. Good for you and the pumpkin."

Tears glistened. She reached out, rubbed the back of his neck. He tensed his shoulders, then relaxed them, and she remembered the condolence letter from a novelist friend of theirs who'd written, "There are no words for this." And she understood that she'd been wrong when she'd thought love could only grow through the accrual of joy. It was deepened by sorrow, the sorrow they felt together and alone. Pain's shadow had begun to recede, but if they lived long enough, it would come again and again.

"Sometimes I'm so afraid," Andrew said.

The music slowed to a beat Hanna could sway to. She draped her arms over his shoulders and rocked him.

"Oh love," she whispered. "Our troubles are just beginning."

ALWAYS A DESCENDANT

∽

Mar Lau wasn't a Buddhist—she wasn't anything, really—but sometimes, if she happened to be passing, she entered the temple on Bowery for her fortune.

On that blindingly hot afternoon in mid-September 1998, an old woman wearing brown slacks and a blue sweater stood before the temple window bowing quickly, over and over, at the statues hidden behind the glassy glare. Mar pushed up her shades, then opened the door.

The coolness inside enveloped her. Strands of smoke streamed from bunched wands of incense. She swallowed, trying hard not to cough. Although the temple interior was lit to full fluorescence, it took her a moment to get used to the lesser brightness. The gilt face of a Buddha emerged. She took a few quick steps across the linoleum, which crackled under her sandals. The sensation of ghost fingers tingled up her spine. Someone was watching her. Turning, she saw several old women, not unlike the woman outside, seated on the benches along the window. The ones not talking stared at her. Nodding once, she turned back toward the altar. Among the crowd of Buddhas and bodhisattvas, the only figure she could accurately identify, by the graceful swoop of her gown and the tipped urn cradled in her arms, was Kuan Yin, the Goddess of Mercy.

One of the old ladies coughed. By now they had her number: *juk sing*, hollow bamboo. She couldn't understand a word they were saying about her. They were, of course, talking about her. The Chinese she knew were shameless that way.

Mar tucked a folded dollar bill into the donation slot. A hundred or so rubber-band-bound scrolls the size of a man's finger lay scattered in the box of fortunes. It was important to choose just the right one, but the ladies had fallen quiet—the better to study her, she thought. Maybe they were eyeing her clothes, black spandex shorts and a tube top under a man's open short-sleeved shirt. Quickly grabbing a fortune, she turned to go, and that's when she saw her.

The old woman was seated slightly apart from the others. An intense stillness emanated from her, a stillness like deep, clear water. She stared straight at Mar. Their gazes locked. For a moment, Mar felt herself fall into those eyes. She was the one who lost the contest, who broke away.

The woman's white hair was so sleek it looked liquid. Instead of the usual sexless polyester, she wore Nikes and a purple running suit made of thin material that gave off a slight sheen. By her regal bearing, Mar guessed she'd once been a great beauty.

Mar nodded hello. The woman blinked, and suddenly she was ordinary—just an old lady among other old ladies, the kind who are invisible when you brush past them on the street.

Outside the temple, Mar walked till she found herself on Canal, the Saturday-afternoon crowd pressing tight around her. In a bucket of clear water an eel shivered. Red snappers and slabs of flayed salmon lay on beds of crushed ice. A windup scuba diver bumped again and again into the side of a white plastic basin. Never before had she seen eyes so fearless. The falling sensation she'd felt staring into their darkness was the same sensation she sometimes felt in bed with men. How could an unknown old woman work on her that way?

In Little Italy, near the garden with the urns, she remembered the scroll in her shirt pocket. Leaning against the chain-link fence, she worked off the rubber band, but stopped short of unrolling the paper. It might not be her true fortune. The ladies in the temple had thrown her off before she could deliberately choose.

She waited for a sign that would tell her whether to toss the fortune or take it to heart, but the hazy-bright sky didn't change and in the garden with the urns, the stone caryatids stared straight ahead, as inexpressive as ever. She twisted the rubber band back on, dropped the scroll into her bag, and continued walking uptown.

The second time she saw the woman, four months later, Mar had just finished eating dim sum with a man she'd slept with the night before.

They had arrived at Hop Shing too late, past noon, and were forced to wait, sweating in their coats near the steam-fogged window, for nearly half an hour. By the time they were seated at one of the large round tables, she and the man, whose name was John, had run out of things to say. The waitresses pushing the stainless-steel carts ignored Mar, who waved and called to get them to stop. John didn't like the turnip cakes or shrimp balls. Too greasy, he said. The ones at Beijing Joe's were better. She almost told him that Beijing Joe's was for white people like him and that this bright, noisy restaurant crowded with Formica tables was the real thing, where as a kid she'd spent countless hours surrounded by grandparents, parents, uncles, cousins, and aunts. Together they'd filled two tables for twelve, no room for strangers.

Looking down at John's hands, at the pitted silver ring on his thumb, she realized he was still a stranger, as much a stranger as the college student seated on her right. Like most of the others, John was a disappointment. Mar was twenty-nine years old, and at times like this she wondered why she still tried. Solitude was nobler and less disconcerting. For weeks, sometimes months, she remained alone. But then loneliness got the better of her, so she would put on her black jeans and go out searching for someone new.

On the corner of Canal, John kissed her, then said he'd call. The night before, lying on her bed with his eyes closed, he had looked like a long-torsoed Christ painted by Rouault. He had been in her life for less than twenty-four hours, and soon he'd be gone.

The Don't Walk sign flashed. Mar stepped into the street. She hadn't slept for more than an hour or two—each time she drifted off, she'd sensed John's presence and startled awake—and in the tunnel vision that exhaustion brings, the woman was a violet blur just beyond her field of focus.

Someone called her full name.

The old woman had stopped in the crosswalk directly in front of her. She didn't seem to notice or mind that the Don't Walk sign was now solid red. She spoke Mar's name again.

"Margaret Lau."

White hair, an unsmiling mouth. She looked vaguely familiar. Having forgotten the day in the temple, Mar couldn't place her. She might have been a relative last seen at a family wedding or funeral two decades ago. After Mar's grandparents died, the thread holding the great-aunts and -uncles and cousins together seemed to dissolve. The dim-sum gatherings grew more infrequent, then stopped. Gradually, without realizing it, Mar forgot. First to fade were the names, then the faces, until she couldn't be sure the people once called family ever really existed. Sometimes, when she wandered through Chinatown, she wondered whether this middle-aged man or that young mother with the sullen girl were related to her. *Relatives. Strangers.* There was no way to know.

She meant to sound polite, but the words came out too fast.

"How do you know me?"

The woman let go of the shopping cart she'd been pushing and held her hands apart. The space between her palms was the length of a loaf of bread. A cab honked, but she ignored it.

"I was at your *gwaat tauh* party," she said. "When you were this big, I held you in my arms."

The dimly lit stairway smelled of fish and burned sesame oil. The woman's purple legs disappeared around the bend in the landing. *Pearl. Aunt Pearl.* Bumping the laden cart up the steps, Mar dredged her memory, but couldn't find anyone named Pearl. Was she the great-aunt who'd complained each time the humidity soared that her hands hurt where the Communists tortured her? Not likely. The English Pearl spoke bore only a hint of a Chinese accent. Hers was the loud, familiar English of Lower Manhattan as spoken by the old Italians and Jews who'd sunk roots deep into the language and claimed it for their own.

Pearl lived on the top floor. The skylight—clouded glass with chicken wire inside—let in enough light to reveal that the upper hallway walls were made of pressed tin. Years ago they might have been cream colored or white, but now the sunken pattern was as black with dirt as the letters etched on old gravestones.

The apartment door stood open. The ceiling of Pearl's kitchen was covered with the same grimy tin. Waist-high stacks of newspapers and *National Geographics* lined the walls. Mar wheeled the cart over the dark red linoleum, which was worn through in spots, like eroded sandstone, to reveal an older layer with yellow flowers.

"Leave that there by the table," Pearl said.

On the board covering the bathtub was a rice cooker, a utensil tray, and a small artificial Christmas tree. The tiny lights strung around the pink branches blinked off and on. Pearl's building was a tenement almost identical to the one Mar lived in on Seventh Street, only in Mar's floor-through the tub in the kitchen seemed stylishly neo-bohemian instead of a relic of the slums. By contrast with Pearl's, her place was almost empty of possessions. A bed, a table, two chairs. A dressmaker's dummy, a boxful of books. Bubble-wrapped paintings she'd made as a student leaned against the walls. Although she'd lived in the apartment for three years, she hadn't finished unpacking.

"Sit," Pearl commanded.

Three of Pearl's four kitchen chairs were covered with piles of envelopes and smoothed-flat plastic bags. On the table were more *National Geographics*, stacks of mustard-colored plates and saucers, a McDonald's cup with a dozen chopsticks in it, and an unopened bag of Stella D'Oro biscotti, the chocolate and vanilla kind.

Mar negotiated the shopping cart between the mountains of saved things, then sat down in the one free chair. She was grateful the apartment was cold enough for her to keep her coat on. She didn't want to display what she wore underneath, black hip-huggers and a scoop-necked knit—modest enough in the New York scheme of things, but too revealing for family.

Pearl lit a match. Blue fire licked the bottom of the dented coffeepot.

"It's fresh," she said. "I made it just before I went out. One cup. That's all the doctor lets me have."

She busied herself with the contents of the cart: bakery boxes, cardboard cartons, bags of greens.

"Can I help?"

Pearl gave her the mock-stern glare of an adult regarding a child who has just said something ridiculous. She opened a carton and quickly, with a pair of chopsticks, picked out choice pieces of soy-sauce duck, which she placed on a dessert plate before Mar.

"Thanks, but I just ate."

As if she hadn't heard, Pearl poured coffee into one of the yellow mugs. "I only got the 2 percent. If you want real milk or cream, too bad."

The duck was salty, moist, rare at the bone. With each bite, Mar found herself sinking deeper into the passivity of childhood. Almost in a dream she remembered sitting at a restaurant table, watching the aunts and uncles talk. That was before she learned there were two languages, and the one she didn't know so well was Cantonese.

Pearl poured milk and spooned sugar into Mar's coffee.

Instead of protesting that she drank it black, Mar took a sip.

"How *do* you know me?" she asked.

"Like I told you already." Pearl held out her arms, cradling an invisible infant. "You cried the whole time. No one knew what to do with you but me."

A half hour later, they sat in the front room of the apartment, Pearl in the green La-Z-Boy, Mar on the edge of the chenille-covered cot she realized must serve as the old woman's bed.

"Everybody wanted me to translate. For Immigration, the mailman, everybody."

Pearl pushed a plate of *baci* and almond cookies, still in their individual cellophane wrappers, across the TV tray toward Mar. She was explaining how she'd been a real catch when she was young. "An American-born Chinese girl, with citizenship papers and everything. You see, we been in America since the Gold Rush days, before Immigration tried to keep us out."

Almost afraid to breathe, Mar waited for Pearl to continue. Her parents didn't like to talk about the past. Chains clacked against metal, a truck lurching by on the cobblestone street below. Glancing at the two front windows, she saw that a shrine stood between them. On the teak table sat a bowl of plastic oranges, a vase of plastic chrysanthemums, and three portraits in wooden frames. The shrine was so perfect she was stricken by the desire to paint it, the first time she'd felt the urge in years.

Following Mar's gaze, Pearl said, "That there's his father. The other big one's my parents." Her eyes filled with keen light. "The last one is my husband. He was your father's Third Uncle."

Mar rose, walked over to the windows. "May I?"

Pearl laughed. "Go right on ahead. They're your ancestors, too."

The portrait of Pearl's father-in-law, Mar's great-grandfather, wasn't a true photo portrait, she realized, but a photograph of a painting. In it, a man in a blue robe sat staring straight ahead. A wispy gray beard and mustache circled his unsmiling mouth.

"He was a warlord with seven wives. Just like the man from St. Ives."

"The man from what?"

"The nursery rhyme. Ain't you ever heard it?" Pearl's eyes went dim with memory. She began to sing:

As I was going to St. Ives
I met a man with seven wives.
Every wife had seven sacks,
Every sack had seven cats,
Every cat had seven kits.
Kits, cats, sacks, and wives,
How many were going to St. Ives?

Slightly embarrassed, Mar kept her eyes on the great-grandfather. The image was familiar. It was, she realized, a reproduction of the almost-life-sized painting that hung in the living room of her grandparents' house in Queens. All through her childhood, the portrait had scared her just enough to render her unable to really see it. But here, on Pearl's table, shrunk down to fit an eight-by-ten frame, her warlord great-grandfather had metamorphosed into a long-faced doll.

She turned to the second portrait, a daguerreotype of a handsome couple in Victorian clothes. The woman was seated, the man standing before a backdrop of painted Grecian ruins. A plaster urn overflowing with ivy had been placed near the woman's chair. She looked angry, but maybe her glare was only the result of the effort to hold still.

"So what's the answer?" Pearl demanded.

"The answer?"

"To the riddle."

"I don't know."

"Think."

Cellophane crackled. Pearl shook the crumbs from the wrappers of the cookies Mar had eaten into one cupped hand. Rising, she sprinkled the crumbs onto the newspaper-lined floor of the birdcage by the La-Z-Boy. Its sole occupant, a white lovebird, hopped down from the perch.

"Treats, Morty." Chuckling, she said, "Only one. Only one of them went to St. Ives. The man, it's always the man. Did they tell you your great-grandpa died young? All those wives outlived him."

The last photo, in black and white, was of a smiling man Mar's age. He wore a coat and fedora, and was stand-ing, one foot a step higher than the other, in the middle of a long flight of marble stairs. The building it led to might have been a courthouse or a monument. The man, who was handsome in a round-faced way, looked like what Mar's mother would call a rake.

"Third Uncle?"

Pearl didn't answer. Mar tried to summon the old men at dim sum who'd given her red envelopes for New Year, but Third Uncle failed to materialize. She had never thought of any of her great-uncles as sexy. The world did not work that way. Besides, when she'd known them, they were old. She had gone to two of their funerals. Staring at the waxy faces below, she had bowed three times, as directed, before the coffins.

"How did you meet?" Mar asked.

The corners of Pearl's mouth turned downward, an expression that meant to say, Who knows? Mar felt the door between them swing shut. She found herself longing to know more about Third Uncle and Pearl's romance, because looking at the photo she knew that love and lust formed the glue that had bound them.

On the way back from the toilet, Mar saw that the second small room past the kitchen had once been the bedroom. Under the shoe boxes and piles of clothes was a full-sized bed draped with the same white chenille that covered Pearl's cot, only this spread was furred with dust. Hanging over the bed was a soft-focus forties-era photograph of a young woman. Lips slightly parted, the woman stared off into the distance. Satin shone against white shoulders. Her wavy hair framed a perfect pale oval—a Modigliani face, only Chinese.

A bar of sandalwood soap lay on a pile of blouses. Mar picked it up, breathed in the sweet scent. Despite the cheesy pose, the woman looked regal. A princess, at least. A queen.

Staring hard, Mar realized where she had seen Pearl before. She laid the soap back down. Her face burned as if with shame. Pearl was the almost-forgotten woman at the temple. For a moment she wondered if, instead of being a relative, Pearl was a madwoman blessed with an intuition for names. Mar had summoned her, the way you can sum-mon crazy people to yourself, because for years she'd half hoped that one day one of those lost aunts or cousins in the Chinatown crowd would recognize her and envelope her once again in family.

The television was on, the sound turned low.

"Is that you? The photo in the bedroom?" Mar asked, knowing it was.

The gleam went out of Pearl's eyes. "No, that's my sister."

A lie.

"She's beautiful."

Pearl shrugged. "So sit down."

"I can't."

"I know. You got things to do." Frowning, Pearl rose from her easy chair.

"Don't get up."

"I got to lock you out, don't I?" She walked swiftly toward the kitchen. Before Mar could say no, Pearl packed several cardboard containers into a pink plastic bag from Maria's Bakery.

"Take this for later," Pearl said. "You're young and skinny. You should eat everything you can before the doctor starts thinking he can run your life."

"I'm not so young."

"Believe me, you're young."

Pearl handed Mar the bag. As if to hasten the inevitable, she now seemed anxious for Mar to leave. She slid the chain free, then began to undo the dead bolts and other locks.

On the landing below, Mar looked back up at Pearl. Lit by the two bare bulbs that hung from the kitchen ceiling, her hair looked as brilliant as buffed steel. The old woman's face was in shadow; only her smooth forehead could be seen.

"Thank you," Mar called. "Thank you for everything."

Pearl was already closing the door. "Didn't they tell you? Family don't thank family," she said and slammed it shut.

The following Monday night, Mar's mother phoned. Mar laid down her chopsticks—dinner was takeout noodles from Teriyaki Boy—then hit the mute on the made-for-television movie she was watching about Joan of Arc. Although she found the movie ridiculous, an MTV version of the life of Saint Joan, she watched because after a long day staring at the computer screen, she was too tired not to.

She and her mother spoke once or twice a week, calls that Mar anticipated more than she liked to admit. She revealed as little as possible about her adult life, yet for the duration of each call she felt bathed in the mild warmth of her mother's voice.

The roof needed new gutters. The doctor said Mar's father's cholesterol was a little higher than it should be. Nothing serious, but it was time he started to watch his heart.

While she listened, Mar thought of Pearl, saw the soft-focus image of Pearl's younger self superimposed on the shadowed old woman's face. She wanted to preserve the mystery that hung like a protective cloud around her aunt, but even more she wanted to disperse that cloud. She had to know exactly how she was connected to the beautiful old woman who, in a city of eight million people, had miraculously found her, then pushed her out the door.

"Mom," she said, "does Dad have an aunt named Pearl?"

Her mother paused. "How did you find out?"

Mar stared at the angel with Michael Bolton hair that

was bursting through a church's stained-glass window. The note of warning in her mother's voice told her she had stepped into taboo territory.

"So Dad *does* have an aunt named Pearl?"

"You still haven't said how you know."

"I bumped into her in Chinatown. Somehow, she recognized me."

For a moment, silence hung between them. Then her mother said, "Third Uncle was a weak man."

"You mean Pearl's husband?"

"He was a weak man. Everyone in the family blames Pearl, but I blame him."

It emerged that Pearl was Third Uncle's second wife. The first wife, left in China for many years, came over after the family finally saved enough money for her passage and papers. When she arrived at her husband's house, Pearl opened the door.

"He hadn't told the wife about Pearl," Mar's mother said. "He hadn't told anyone. I can't imagine what he was thinking."

During the time it took to save for her fare back to Guangdong, Third Uncle's first wife stayed with Mar's grandparents. Every day she told them, in language that grew more vivid as the months wore on, what lowlifes the Laus were.

"That's when your father decided he didn't want a family when he grew up. An extended family, I mean."

Saint Joan stared tremblingly at the window the angel had just destroyed. She was a wispy actress, a blond Kate Moss. The real Joan had been a farm girl likely endowed with iron muscles from the daily round of chores.

"Don't mention Pearl to your father. Leave her in the past."

Although she'd just been told never to see her great-aunt again, Mar promised. She also promised, before saying good-bye, to come to Port Washington soon.

Her noodles had grown cold. Now dressed in a mail vest, Joan stared into a full-length mirror. She unsheathed her knife. In the next shot, strands of long, pale hair fell to the floor. Mar understood why Third Uncle hadn't breathed a word about Pearl even though it seemed insane to keep the fact of her hidden. He had been ashamed. Pearl was his secret, his sin against family. When he was with her, he eased into another life, a life that was his alone.

Mar paced the length of her narrow apartment, wondering about the woman who had caused so much trouble. Pearl might live like a recluse, but in her time she had taken risks. By choosing a married man, she had defied the constraints of her time to get exactly what she wanted. She was a sexual outlaw, a hero. Even now she didn't care who thought what of her. Most women her age produced pictures of children and grandchildren, as if those children and grandchildren were the reason for their existence—but Pearl lived for herself, it seemed.

Mar found the remote, turned the television off. She, too, was a kind of outlaw. Maybe Pearl had sensed their connection.

Because she wasn't in the mood to talk to men, she pulled her hair into a tight bun and wore a loose white blouse, her don't-touch-me look. Caryn wasn't the type of woman who drew fire, so they were safe.

Caryn stirred her martini with a tiny red swizzle stick shaped like a sword.

"So you found the family's black sheep," she said.

Circles of light shining from the small holes in the

ceiling dotted Caryn's hands. It was ten o'clock, and Global's bar was two deep with people Mar and Caryn's age or younger. *Black sheep.* Mar hadn't thought of Pearl that way, although the label made sense. While her pride erased any tint of disgrace, it was true she was an outcast.

"Did Pearl and your father's uncle ever actually get married?"

Mar thought for a second. "You know, I don't really know."

"What about children?"

"She didn't mention any."

Briefly wondering why she hadn't asked, Mar looked across the table at her friend's square-chinned face. She was the kind of woman other women called attractive, the decent, mildly boring kind Mar always seemed to befriend. Soon enough, the conversation turned to war stories. Caryn's boyfriend of eight years was stalling about marriage again. Although he worked as a legal copyeditor, he thought of himself as a poet. He needed his privacy to write. They didn't exactly live together, but spent Saturday and Wednesday nights at Caryn's apartment.

"I've been thinking about an ultimatum. You know, a deadline." Caryn laughed unhappily. "Paul knows all about deadlines."

Paul had been given ultimatums before, yet nothing had changed. Mar wondered why marriage was considered such a big deal. Why yearn for an institution, especially one so hard on women?

"Single women live longer, so the studies say," Mar said.

"Thanks a lot."

Caryn leaned down to sip from her glass, which was

filled to the lip. "Your turn now." Her eyes gleamed with interest. Part of Mar's job as her friend was to entertain.

"No one new, not really. Just some fool who thought he knew more about *siu mai* than me."

She didn't want to think about John, the man she'd picked up last weekend, but by the same measure talking could exorcise the bitter edge of failure surrounding his already faint memory. He worked in a chain bookstore, in the reference and how-to section. A tedious, low-paying job, but look at the fringe benefits, he said. Back at her apartment they tore her bottom bedsheet, probably when one or the other of them hooked a finger or toe into the burn hole left by a careless cigarette. Although on first impression he seemed gentle, in the final analysis John was thoughtless and arrogant. He hadn't apologized about the sheet or had the courtesy to pick up the used condoms. When Mar returned from Chinatown to her ruined bed, she'd found two of them sealed to the wooden floor like flaps of moist skin.

"Think you'll see him again?"

The woman at the next table, whose blond hair was braided into tight cornrows, started to laugh.

"No way in the world," Mar said.

Telling Caryn the story hadn't helped. Emptiness was the price paid for sleeping with someone she barely knew. What kept her coming back was the spark that sometimes flashed, burning away all sense of strangeness. She imagined that mothers gazing into the faces of their just-born babies might feel the same ecstasy of recognition.

The cornrow woman carefully watched the lips of the man she was with. Mar could tell she wasn't really interested in what he was saying. Smoothing the water-spotted paper that covered her and Caryn's table, she studied the rings of light that played over her hands.

"Sometimes I wonder about the whole business," she said. "Maybe I'll become a hermit. An anchoress."

"A what?"

"It's like being a nun."

"You?"

"Is the idea so odd?"

She thought of Pearl insulated by piles of newspaper, magazines, the crush of read and unread words. Pearl was a true hermit, one of those urban hermits who managed to remain alone. Although Mar wasn't that extreme, she valued solitude, too. Caryn, her closest friend, had never seen her apartment. Mar's parents had only visited once. True, she brought men home, but none of them stayed.

Caryn was laughing. "In your dreams."

Mar ran her finger down the columns of Laus, pausing for a moment at her own name, M. Lau, no address listed. The ambiguity of the "M" was meant to disguise her gender, but the naked initial practically announced, as obscene phone callers knew, that she was a woman living alone.

Her finger stopped. *Pearl J. Lau.* No useless subterfuges for her. Mar punched the number in quickly, before she could think. The phone rang eleven times, twelve. Disappointed, she hung up. Without knowing it, she had expected Pearl to remain where she'd left her, standing in the bare-bulb glare of her grim kitchen—as if time stopped for her, starting again only when Mar reentered her life.

She called again an hour later, and again after she returned from doing errands. At seven, Pearl finally picked up. The voice that said hello sounded shakier and deeper than Mar remembered. It could as easily have belonged to a man as to a woman.

"Who's there?"

The voice was harsh, accusing. Mar couldn't speak. She had to collect her wits fast, before Pearl mistook *her* for an obscene phone caller and hung up.

"It's me," she said softly. "Margaret. Your grand-niece."

Pearl, if it was Pearl, was the silent one now. Through the earphone, Mar heard the broken wail of a siren.

"We met last weekend. You had me up to your apartment."

"You think I don't know who you are? You're Robert's girl, the one who's the artist."

"I'm not really an artist. I work in a graphics design . . ."

"You're an artist."

It was a mistake. Mar secretly longed for the relatives vanished from her life, but now, hearing the angry resistance in Pearl's voice, she understood why her father avoided them. However, she couldn't back down now. She'd started this and would have to carry the moment through to its end.

"I was wondering if you were free tomorrow. For dim sum."

The siren on Pearl's end grew fainter. "I got things to do."

"What things?"

"A million things."

Mar closed her eyes. She was off the hook, it seemed. Then she remembered she didn't want to be off the hook. She had found Pearl and, despite a misgiving or two, wanted to keep her.

"What about next week?"

Waiting for the answer, Mar glanced again at the phone book filled with Laus. There were so many of them. So many of *us*, she corrected herself.

Pearl cleared her throat, then said, "Fine. Come to Sunday supper."

"Supper? I didn't mean to invite my . . ."

"Six o'clock," Pearl snapped. "See you then."

Although Christmas was over by almost a month, green garlands hung across Mulberry Street like scraggly feather boas. It was freezing cold. Particles of frost glittered in the pink glow around the streetlights. Two days before, the Year of the Ox had begun. In the plastic bags Mar carried were a bunch of red carnations and a box of miniature cannoli. She knew she should bring oranges, too, but she'd forgotten how many meant good luck. Odd or possibly even numbers were bad. She didn't dare call home to ask, because asking would mean she no longer knew. Besides, her mother would want to know why the information was suddenly so vital.

She crossed Canal. Carp and catfish moved slowly through the green water of the fish tank in the Ocean Treasure Restaurant. In the window of a jewelry store stood a pair of black-felt-covered hands. The neon sign above shone red. The only characters she could read were *dai* and *jung*, "big" and "middle." Middle meant China, the center of the world. The mystery of Chinatown was the mystery of family. On which street had her father been born? The ghosts of great-uncles and -aunts, living and dead, mingled with the evening crowd. Were any besides Pearl still alive? What about their children and children's children? Was the woman with the thin face and black coat a cousin? All Mar had to do was call out the right name, but she didn't know any names. *Dai* and *jung* got her nowhere.

Mar reached into her coat pocket, pulled out the scrap of paper with Pearl's address, and checked it against the number in chipped gold above the front door. She scanned the names beside the buzzers, dismayed to see they were all in Chinese. Pearl's last name, *Lau*, her own name, meant "willow." When she was ten or eleven, her grandmother had written the ideogram for her. "Can you see the branches?" she'd asked. Mar hadn't seen the branches then and couldn't now. She pushed the bottom button and waited for the answering buzz that might unlock the door.

It didn't come. An old woman walking by with slowly rocking steps turned to stare. Mar pushed the button again. The brick front of the building was dark with the soot of decades. She wondered if she should try the other buzzers or just give up.

At last, a white-haired head jutted from a top-floor window. Without a word Pearl flung a small white bundle into the air. Mar watched it plummet like a dead dove to land with a thud at her feet. It was an envelope folded into a square, tightly wrapped with two crossed rubber bands. Inside, on a Tweety Bird key chain, were a long brass key and four shorter keys, three silver and one gold. Mar looked up at the window for guidance, but Pearl was gone.

The gold key fit the downstairs lock. The hallway was darker, the stairs steeper than she remembered. On the sixth and last floor, Mar knocked. The metal door, painted a deep red, seemed to absorb the sound. No answer. She knocked again. Nothing. Maybe the keys meant she was supposed to let herself in. Turning the brass key in the top lock, she felt the resistance of someone on the other side turning, too. The other locks clicked, small firecracker explosions, and the door creaked open.

"Hold your horses. I was watching the news."

Pearl had changed out of the purple running suit into fitted black slacks and a red silk blouse. Large round earrings made to look like mother-of-pearl—or maybe they were real mother-of-pearl—weighed down her lobes.

The kitchen table was also transformed. The stacks of bills had been cleared away, and in their place were a dozen or more bowls and steamer trays. Sliced pork, dumplings, noodles. The rice cooker's red eye glowed like a small animal's.

Mar placed her box of pastry on the seat of one empty chair. Two of them, she saw, were now cleared for sitting.

"I brought you these," she said, holding out the carnations.

"The news is almost over."

Mar followed Pearl into the front room. The TV was filled with the image of Monica Lewinsky, dark eyes shining with adoration or love.

"Men are all the same. Especially when they get a little power," Pearl murmured.

She reached up to adjust one earring. Remembering how she used to play with her mother's clip-on earrings when she was a kid, Mar could almost feel the bite of the clamp on tender flesh.

"They think they rule the world," Pearl was saying. "I don't know why I bother to watch. There's no news, just the same old story over and over."

Mar, who had no patience for the Lewinsky case—of what significance was it where the man put his dick? she'd told Caryn—offered the carnations again. Pearl's face brightened, as if she was seeing the flowers for the first time.

"Roses," she said.

"They're carnations."

"Tea roses. My favorite."

Embarrassed by her own stinginess—why hadn't she spent a few extra dollars for some roses?—Mar didn't correct her again.

While they ate in the kitchen, Pearl told Mar the names— in English, then slowly, in Cantonese—of each dish she set before her. So the rubbery strands she devoured at family banquets were dried jellyfish. From the age of six or seven on, she was ashamed to ask—ashamed because she was supposed to know, just as she was supposed to know the family names of each of the old people at dim sum. There was the aunt whose thumbs had been twisted by the Communists, and the uncle—Fourth Uncle?—whose tremendous mole covered half his forehead. Most of the others lacked distinguishing marks. After the first greeting, during which they patted and pinched her cheeks and the women checked behind her ears to see if they'd been washed, the old people rarely spoke to her. And when they did, it was in the language she understood less and less with each passing year.

Freed from its cage, the lovebird perched on Pearl's shoulder. White and gray shit streaked the cloth draped over her shoulder. They had reached the final course, noodles for long life. Pearl tucked in her chin so as to look at the bird.

"You been a good boy, Morty," she said gently. "You hungry?"

Round black eyes glittering, the bird tilted its head,

then hopped onto Pearl's outstretched finger. She took a noodle into her mouth, held it between her lips. With a twinge of dread Mar watched the bird snap the noodle up. Small body quivering, it ruffled its feathers with pleasure.

"He loves noodles," Pearl said.

"Is that the way you always feed him?"

"Why not? That's the way the mothers feed their babies."

The intimacy of the gesture disturbed Mar. This was the first time Pearl seemed weird to her, twisted by loneliness into committing strange acts of love.

"You like him?" Pearl asked.

Mar glanced at the tiny eyes, which now seemed to gleam with malevolence. "He seems nice," she said.

"Take him."

Before she could object, Pearl settled the lovebird onto the front of Mar's sweater. Its claws rasped against the black sequins, trying to find a hold. While Mar froze, it scrabbled up her chest to her shoulder, where it hid in hollow of her neck, sheltered by her long hair.

Pearl's face was soft with elation. "He likes you."

The bird was so light Mar almost didn't feel him, just the slight pressure of his claws and ticklish brush of his nervously turning head.

"Lovebirds live longer than we do. Morty's just a baby. He has a long life ahead."

"That's good."

Pearl nodded. "We'll take dessert in the living room."

"What about Morty?"

"Just get up and walk normal. He can go anywhere you can."

As they passed through the abandoned bedroom, Mar

stole a glimpse of the portrait of Pearl. The young woman gazing off into the distance seemed slightly less beautiful than she'd remembered, the cheeks wider, the eyes less large. What would the woman in the picture have thought of the woman Pearl had become?

The soft click, click was Morty pecking at her dangling earring, which was made of red glass. Pearl bent over the TV tray. She undid the tight knot on Mar's bakery box, unraveled the red-and-white string, and carefully wrapped it around her palm, like a pugilist taping his fist. When she opened the lid, she appraised the sugar-dusted cannoli as if Mar had brought her precious jewels.

"Good," she said. "You got the chocolate. They're the only kind I eat."

After they finished, Pearl stared at the TV screen, watching Joie Chen's deadpan face. Her own face was expressionless. It was as if Mar wasn't there.

"Should I go?" Mar asked.

"Sit."

She was already seated, on the edge of the cot. Back in his cage, Morty listlessly pecked at a thin slab of salt or bone. Joie Chen was saying something about more than fifty Asians found dead in Dover. The bodies were discovered in the back of a truck on a ship that had crossed the Channel. Some of the men appeared to have suffocated, while others may have been killed to shield the identity of the person or persons who'd attempted to smuggle them into the country.

"What a shame," Mar said, to break the silence.

Her voice seemed to startle Pearl out of a dream. "What's the shame? It's been going on for years. Only now they're making a big deal."

"But all those dead?"

Pearl twisted in her chair to face her. "How do you think your family got here?"

"I assumed . . ."

"Ten thousand dollars," she said. "Ten thousand dollars apiece. That was a lot of money in those days. Still is." Pearl hit the mute button, and the TV went silent. "They made me translate. I was the only one who could speak good American."

Mar glanced at the shrine—at her carnations, now jammed into the white glass vase, at her eternally young Third Uncle, and at the warlord great-grandfather in his Virgin Mary–blue robe.

"My father never talked much about the family," she said.

Pearl nodded. "Robert was always that way. A modern boy."

"In fact, I'm not even sure where everyone is. Do they still live in Chinatown?"

"Some. Some moved to Sunset Park. The young ones are all over the place, like you."

"Do you stay in touch?"

Pearl's eyes flickered with doubt. She shrugged, then looked at Morty, who had turned his head sideways to gnaw on one of the cage's bars. "These days I got a million things to do."

Mar rose from the cot. She felt ashamed for having asked the question, since she'd already known the answer. "Well," she said, "I ought to be going."

Pearl laid her hands on the arms of the La-Z-Boy. "I know. You got work tomorrow."

Before Mar could say another word, Pearl strode through the apartment. In the kitchen, she took a stack of ricotta-cheese containers out of the cupboard. With a fresh pair of chopsticks, she whisked the pork into a quart-sized cup. Watching, Mar realized she had already forgotten the name of each dish.

"Can I help?"

Pearl glared at her. She shook two plastic shopping bags open and began to pile the yellow containers into them.

"You've got to keep some," Mar said, when she realized what Pearl was doing. "After all the trouble you . . ."

"Not with this heart. My doc would kill me." She put in the last container, filling the bag. "I'm taking some noodles for Morty, that's all."

Mar thought of her own refrigerator, the tiny, doorless freezer caked with ice, the takeout cartons, the jam jars crusted with mold. With whom could she share this bounty? Caryn? Their friendship played itself out under the dim lights of the trendy bar or restaurant of the moment. Her parents? She couldn't see herself on the Long Island Railroad surrounded by the richly reeking bags like some old Chinese lady. Whenever she went home to visit, she brought *bao* or cannoli, antiseptically tucked into white bakery boxes, no odor to betray her.

Helplessly, Mar said, "Then, thank you. Thank you so much."

Pearl stared at her, in mock chagrin. "Do I got to tell you every time? You don't thank family."

"But I . . ."

"Go," Pearl said.

Mar put on her coat, then lifted the bags. Twelve containers, one for each course. At the bottom of one bag lay the cannoli box, retied with the red-and-white string, as if it had never been opened.

Feeling in her pocket for her wallet, Mar removed the

envelope that enfolded Pearl's keys. "These are yours," she said.

"Keep them. I got another extra set."

"You sure?"

"Sure I'm sure. It's easier than throwing them out the window."

This was Pearl's way of saying she could come back. Mar wanted to hug her old aunt, but looking into her stern face, she didn't know how.

"Well," she said, *"Gung hei fat choi."*

Happy New Year, or, more accurately, *All best wishes for good money.* It was the only phrase she still remembered without having to dredge through the sad chaos of a half-forgotten language.

Now Pearl did smile, clearly amused. *"Lei si dou loih,"* she said and closed the door.

Back in her own apartment on Seventh Street, Mar was too wound up to sleep. She had found her black sheep, the woman who might be the key to the past her father hoped to leave behind. She got out of bed, unearthed a container of *siu mai,* and took it into the living room. The Robin Byrd Show was on. A woman, naked except for stilettos and a red G-string, crossed her arms under tremendous spherical breasts. The skin on them, stippled with green veins, looked stretched so tight it might burst.

An ad came on. A woman in a bikini rubbed lotion onto the thonged thigh of a second woman with Farrah Fawcett hair. "Why be lonely tonight?" a voice intoned. "Call Big Apple Escorts."

Mar switched to the Weather Channel. Icicles glistened on the drooping arc of a power line. The *siu mai* were delicious. Pearl had tried to instruct Mar in their making. "Easy," she'd said. "Put the pork, sherry, water chestnuts, soy sauce, and MSG into the blender." When Mar asked how much of each ingredient, Pearl thought for a moment, then said, "Enough." As for the dumpling skins—her voice rose, for emphasis—"Don't make them, buy them. Who got time for all that trouble?"

Words of wisdom. She wondered what else she stood to learn from Pearl.

The following Sunday, she went with Pearl to Hop Shing. They arrived at ten o'clock and, for a moment, had a table to themselves. Pearl ordered noodles and congee, the richly flavored pabulum Mar hadn't eaten since she was a child. Sipping it with her soup spoon, she remembered— a memory so strong it felt as real as someone pinching her arm—gazing up into the old people's faces while they talked, ate, and ignored her.

Pearl kept quiet. Instead of speaking, she nodded imperiously to the waitresses, who always paused to see if she might want the dishes on their carts. When she and Mar ran out of tea, Pearl opened the lid of the stainless-steel teapot, which was whisked away and returned full.

Instead of speaking this time, Mar kept quiet, too. It was peaceful, she found, to not have to talk, and so it was with a slight stab of regret that she finally asked, after they'd eaten their egg custards, if Pearl would tell her more about the family.

"Got a pen?" Pearl pushed the empty plates and saucers away from her place. Unfolding a clean napkin, she smoothed the creases flat, then traced a single ideogram.

"That's our name," she said. Mar saw in the radical's strokes a straight trunk and branches reaching out and down. *Lau. Willow.* Their name *was* a tree, a strong, graceful tree. Now that she saw it, she wondered why she'd been unable to see it before.

"Your grandfather was the first son."

Watching the lines emerge, Mar asked, "Is that his real name or his paper name?"

Pearl scowled. "He thought his word was like Moses. Always trying to run people's lives."

Mar remembered her grandfather as a kind man who smelled of White Owl cigars. Whenever he saw Mar, he smiled with the purest joy she'd ever seen on an adult face and pulled her close to sing, in his heavily accented English, "You Are My Sunshine."

Looking at his name, which seemed hopelessly complex to her, Mar said, "How do you pronounce it?"

"Ah-Cheun."

"What does it mean?"

Pearl shrugged.

"Can you write his name in English, too? The transliteration, I mean."

The wary look in Pearl's eyes alerted Mar to her mistake.

"You write it," Pearl said.

"I only have one pen, and you've got it in your hand."

"You're smart, you went to college. You can remember." Pearl began to write a third character. "This is Second Uncle."

She kept writing and reciting names till she'd finished the generation. Altogether, there were four sons and five daughters. Now she began to draw dashes connecting each name to a new ideogram.

"The husbands and wives," she said. "That's me, Ah-Jyu. 'Pearl' in American."

She paused to grin at Mar. "If I was old-fashioned,

I'd write it messed up and small. You're not supposed to write your own name nice." Her eyes glittered—with mischief, Mar thought. "I don't go in for that stuff. I was born here and got the papers to prove it. They can say what they like."

Mar smiled back. They understood each other, she thought. Although almost fifty years separated them—by Mar's calculations Pearl had to be at least in her seventies—they were the same kind of woman. They were both fighters.

More names blossomed on the page: the next generation, the children.

"That there's your father. First son of the first son. The fuss they made when he was born."

Uncles, aunts, and second cousins filled the napkin. When Pearl drew a line extending down from her own name, Mar felt a twinge of surprise. She hadn't expected Pearl to have children. But of course she did. Everyone did, in those days.

"My daughter, Dolores," Pearl intoned.

"Where is she now?"

"Florida." Pearl raised her head to look meaningfully at Mar. "I hate Florida. It's where old people go to die."

"Do you have grandchildren?"

"Be quiet and watch."

She drew two lines from her daughter's name. "A boy and a girl, Arthur and Carol. Dolores didn't give them no Chinese names."

"What about her husband? Is he Chinese?"

"We don't talk about him." Without looking, Pearl laid down the pen in a pool of spilled tea. The light in her eyes faded. "Men," she said. "They're all the same. No, they're not the same—some are even worse."

If Pearl had been Caryn, Mar would have been at no loss for words, but now she didn't know what to say. She picked up the pen, wiped it dry on her leggings. A waiter appeared, stacked the plates, and counted them, quickly touching each with a fingertip. He wrote out the bill, then set it on the table. Pearl stared at his departing back.

"Be careful who you marry."

"I'm not getting married anytime soon. Maybe never," Mar said softly.

"Watch out for the ones who promise they'll change."

"OK, I will." She rose from the table, the bill in one hand. "You stay here while I pay, Aunt Pearl."

Beads of water trickled down the steam-fogged windows. When Mar returned, a couple had been seated at their table with them. She was Chinese, he was white, and by the close yet inattentive way they sat together Mar could see they had been lovers for a while. The man glanced at Mar, a quick appraisal. Pearl was again writing ideograms on the napkin, which had torn in places where she'd pressed down too hard.

Without looking up from her labors, she said, "I don't know your mother's Chinese name." She wrote in "Ann," then drew one line down from the hyphen that joined Mar's parents.

"That's you," she said. "They made a fuss over you, too. Your grandfather said, 'This is America. She should have a *gwaat tauh*, even if she is a girl.' You should have seen the food."

Pearl held her hands apart. "This big. You cried your head off. I was the only one that could make you stop." Her fingers trembled slightly, as if she still felt the swaddled heat given off by the infant Mar had been.

She resumed writing. "This is your name." Mar stared

down at the two characters. She knew she'd been given a Chinese name, but had never seen it written before.

"What does it mean?"

Pearl studied the napkin. "What do you call it when someone's a child? A child of the ancestors."

Across the table, the white man drummed his fingers against the woman's thin wrist. They were both in their mid-twenties. A circle of pale green jade hung from an almost invisible gold chain around her neck. She hadn't once acknowledged Mar, and Mar thought she knew why. Shame. She was ever so slightly ashamed to be sitting across from Mar and Pearl, who were the very vision of the good girl and her grandmother.

"You went to college, you know the word," Pearl was saying.

"I *don't* know. A descendant?"

Pearl's mouth widened into a smile. "Yeah, that's it. Your name means 'always a descendant,' 'always a Lau.'" She tucked an escaped wing of white hair behind her ear. "Your grandfather named you. I guess he didn't want you to forget."

The first time Mar tried to repeat the inflected syllables, Pearl laughed. "No, no, no. Listen. Watch." She pronounced the name more slowly, exaggerating each liquid tonal rise and fall. Mar tried again, and again Pearl laughed. Then her face grew serious. She spoke the name patiently, over and over, until Mar got it right.

Mar took to eating Sunday supper with Pearl. The habit had some effect on her love life because deep down she didn't want her Pearl Sundays, as she secretly called them, to be disturbed. Later she would understand Pearl Sundays were one reason why, in April, she took up with

Curt, who was married. With a married man, she could count on a kind of stability.

When he dropped his MetroCard in the Astor Place station and she called out after him, she liked how his angry eyes softened when he saw her. Soon he was coming to her apartment almost every Thursday, just after eight. She loved his fast-talking energy and the burned, slightly bitter taste of his mouth. He arrived too wired to sit still. After a brief, hard kiss he paced her living room and talked about the fools and geniuses who populated his days. It was breathtaking how much money there was to be lost or made in trading. Eventually he lay down with her on the couch. He was a surprisingly slow and gentle lover. By the time he was ready to leave, at eleven, no later than eleven-thirty, his muscular, pale body was as peaceful as the body of an infant who has finally given in to sleep.

After he left, Mar would settle into deep, restful slumber. One good thing about Curt was she didn't have to sleep with him. She'd never been able to sleep well with someone else in her bed.

At the beginning of a relationship—any relationship, whether the man was married or not—she often was filled with a longing so urgent it bordered on pain. She tried her best to mask the longing with casualness, but the man could smell it and was flattered, moved, or, more often, repelled. With Curt, though, she felt oddly content. The phone calls and weekly visits were enough.

April bled into May. The summer passed, and he still came to her every Thursday. She told Caryn, who instead of reveling in Mar's exploits scolded her. "What if you were *her*?" she said. "It's not like that," Mar answered. What she wanted to say was this was practically the longest she'd been with anyone. Although she didn't exactly love him, she wished she could tell her mother about Curt. She wished she could tell Pearl. One day it occurred to her that perhaps she could. After all, Third Uncle had been someone else's husband, too.

Across the table from Mar, Pearl worked silently on her plate of calamari and linguini. They were at La Foccaceria on First Avenue because it was time, Mar said, that they eat in her territory for a change.

Pearl's eyes were filled with a distant look of pleasure. A strand of linguini fell from her fork, leaving a snaky red streak on the bosom of her running suit.

"How did you meet? You and Third Uncle, I mean," Mar asked.

Pearl paused, forkful of tentacled calamari held in midair. "How does anyone meet anyone? At work, your grandfather's restaurant. Louie—I called him Louie— was one of the waiters. I was the hostess, which meant I caught all the trouble."

She put the calamari in her mouth, chewed. Mar waited. Pearl finally laid down her fork and said, "Wherever I worked, I was always the hostess because I knew American. You should have seen the silk dresses I wore. Princess cut. So tight I couldn't sit down."

"You must have looked very beautiful."

Pearl grinned. "You know how Chinese people eat family style. Americans eat separate. Each American ate their own dish, so the waiters had to remember who ordered what."

The busboy, a young Mexican man with a topknot pulled back in a queue, poured them more water. An ice cube clattered onto the table. Pearl glared. "Pour from the side of the pitcher, that doesn't happen," she said.

"Sorry."

She didn't answer. Mar smiled at him, *Humor her*, but he didn't catch her eye. After he walked away, Pearl said, "Louie couldn't remember. So he'd know where to put the plate, he wrote next to each order 'fat woman' or 'bald man with mole.' It used to give me a laugh."

"What was he like? Third Uncle, Louie?" What made you love him? Mar wanted to ask.

"Like?" Pearl shrugged. "What's any man like?"

Guadalupe, the waitress, who usually bantered with Mar when she came to La Foccaceria alone, paused at their table. "How are you ladies doing? Ready for coffee? Dessert?"

"Coffee," Pearl said, without looking up.

"Espresso?"

"No, the regular."

"Nothing for me. Thanks, Lupe." Mar smiled again, trying to compensate for her dour aunt. The red sauce stain on the synthetic fabric of Pearl's running suit had grown darker, more soaked in. Her manners, or lack of them, which seemed acceptable, even appropriate, in Chinatown, now made Mar cringe.

Pearl chuckled. "My second cup today," she said. "Don't tell my doctor, he'd have a heart attack."

Mar thought that the fleeting story about Third Uncle was all she would hear that day on the subject of men, but when the coffee came, Pearl looked her in the eye.

"Remember what I say," she said. "Men are men. The young ones are more trouble than they're worth, and the old ones sit around all day with their gossip."

She ripped open two packets of sugar, then poured in the cream. "Your grandfather was the worst. When your third uncle and I wanted to save for Dolores's college, he said, 'No, the money goes to the family.' He thought his word was the word of God. Like he forgot this was America."

After Mar paid the bill, they walked slowly down Seventh Street. She paused in front of her apartment building, for a moment seeing the whitewashed façade as if for the first time.

"Here's where I live. Want to come up? I've got some biscotti for dessert."

Pearl shook her head. Her cheeks sagged against the collar of her gray raincoat. "No, I gotta get home. Morty needs his supper."

They walked to Second Avenue so Pearl could catch the bus. While they stood in the kiosk, it began to drizzle. Someone had graffitied over the poster encased in one Plexiglas wall so that the eyes of the very thin, very young model were as wide as Krazy Kat's. Pearl's hair was misted with tiny stars of rain. Feeling a wave of tenderness, Mar fished through her bag, found her spare keys, and pressed them into Pearl's gloved hand.

"You know where I live. Use them," she said.

Pearl closed her hand around the keys. The bus stopped before her, then flung open its doors. Without looking at Mar, she climbed on. Stung, Mar thought Pearl had missed the meaning of her gesture, but just before the doors closed, she turned and said, "Good-bye, dear."

Mar almost laughed. It was the first time Pearl had ever called her "dear," the first time she'd said "good-bye."

After weeks of almost unnatural summery heat, bitter cold lashed the city. When Mar emerged from the Astor Place station, freezing air tingled against her cheeks. Instead of picking up some takeout and heading home, she decided to walk. The prospect of returning to her overheated apartment alone depressed her. If there was a season of loneliness, it was fall.

Walking past the Radio Bar on First Avenue, she peered through the window. The lit-up jukebox looked as if it was floating underwater, but she didn't feel strong enough to go inside. On vulnerable nights like this, the men she drew could be scary, obsessed with Asians or the idea of women as defenseless children.

She wasn't really hungry either, so she stopped at Porto Rico for some coffee. Sipping as she walked, she found herself in front of St. Mark's Church, the austere spire luminous in the floodlights. Sitting on the stone foundation of the fence was the woman Mar sometimes gave change to. No matter what the weather, she wore layers of skirts, like petticoats, one over the other. She was different from other panhandlers because—was it the way she met the giver's eyes?—Mar could imagine her in another life.

"God bless." The woman smiled up at Mar, not even glancing at the two quarters she'd placed in her coffee cup.

A striped canopy tent was pitched on the cobblestones. Underneath were tables on which lay open boxes of apples, their skins as lustrous as pewter. Sweet, spiced steam poured from the mouth of a large crockpot. Hot cider. Thinking of stone cellars and orchards dusted with frost, Mar walked over to the farm stand.

Reaching up, she pulled down a plastic bag, then tore it along the perforated line. Glancing at the man behind the tables, Mar sensed more than saw that he was handsome. She looked closer, liking the line of his chin and the black curly hair that sprang from under his watch cap. He was looking at her, too, so she smiled and made a show of rubbing her arms.

"Cold," she said. "Too cold to be standing out here."

"Want to know my survival secret?"

Taking a step closer, she saw that he was her age or a few years older.

"Sure."

"Think Costa Rica. Think Yucatán. That, and wear layers."

She laughed. "So what do you have for me?"

"Depends on what you want." The words, flirtatious enough, were delivered with dead seriousness. "The Empires, the Galas, all of these"—he waved one arm over the boxes of fruit—"are sweet and good for eating. The Romes are for baking, if you like to bake."

"That's not in my vocabulary." She tried to whip open the bag, but couldn't get the plastic membranes apart.

"Might help if you had two hands," he said, taking the coffee cup from her.

He wore gloves without fingertips. The fingers that briefly touched hers felt rough and cool.

"If you like your coffee black, keep it. You need it more than me." When he hesitated, she added, "Don't worry, I don't have any diseases. And I'm no Lucrezia Borgia."

"I didn't think you were." He ladled cider into a second takeout cup, blue with white Ionic columns. "Let's call it a trade."

She tasted cloves, cinnamon, an unexpected whiff of bay leaf. Their breath made frost clouds as they talked. The farm, his family's, was in Mt. Hope, New Jersey. Matthew—his name was Matthew—came to the city twice a week, for this farmers' market and the one at Tompkins Square Park. It was a busy life, but not so bad in the winter. A few years ago, he'd been a computer programmer, and before that—well, maybe he'd tell her about it someday. He had gone back to the farm to help while his father recovered from bypass surgery. That was two years ago, he said, grinning.

"Truth is I prefer this work. It took me awhile to figure out, though. Guess I had to leave the farm before I could learn how to come back."

Although the things he said were ordinary enough, his words seemed charged and alive. She didn't know if it was because she wanted him or because he was genuine. She set down her cup on the edge of the table. It was time to leave. She had to blow her nose and didn't want to rake through her bag for last winter's used tissues with him watching.

"Well," she said, "I'd better get going."

He reached over, picked up her cider cup, and tucked it inside the now-empty takeout cup of coffee. "I'm coming to the city again on Thursday. No apple cart this time. Would you like to have dinner?"

Nodding, she reached into her wallet for a business card. Glancing at the company logo, an abstract school of fish diving into the blue pool of a computer screen, she suddenly felt foolish. "This is where I work. I have the kind of job that's just a job."

"That's no crime."

"You can call me there."

"I will."

Like a young girl who's just been kissed, Mar longed to flee. "Talk to you soon," she said, turning away.

One hand in her bag, she groped for tissues, found instead the tightly wrapped scroll of the unread fortune she'd gotten at the Buddhist temple the day she'd first seen Pearl. She reached the curb, but he was shouting after her, calling her by her full first name. Surprised that he knew—the only other person who called her Margaret was Pearl—she spun around. In one hand, he held her card, in the other the bag of apples she'd paid for and forgotten: the sweet kind, good for eating.

"I believe these are yours."

"Shit," she whispered, and walked back to him.

Mar kissed Matthew's throat, then unbuttoned the top button of his shirt. They were lying on her bed. The room was washed in the warm glow of the reading lamp. In that merciful light, the unclothed dressmaker's dummy stand-ing in the corner looked almost alive.

"Wait," he murmured, "there's something I have to tell you."

Stung by sadness, she looked into his eyes. The brown irises contracted as if she'd touched them. She liked him, so much it scared her. Don't talk, don't say a word, she wanted to say. What was his secret? A communicable disease, a lover, a wife? Mar let go of his shirt, which was made of soft brown flannel. It probably wasn't a wife. Men with wives told you from the start or didn't tell at all.

Leaning on one elbow, he traced the arc of skin above her blouse.

"So smooth," he said. Then he said, "You could say I've had many incarnations. I don't know if you would've recognized me ten years ago."

He sat up facing her, so she sat up, too. "When I was younger and stupider than I am now, I had a great idea." He finished unbuttoning his shirt, shrugged out of the sleeves, then pulled off his T-shirt. A dark blotch covered his body. She looked, then looked away, as shocked as if she'd seen the stump of a missing limb. When she looked again, the darkness had become a tattoo of a skeleton, beautifully rendered, almost as large as life. The skull's empty sockets stared at her from his chest.

"Meet Memento Mori. There's more to him. You'll see if I ever finish the strip show."

Matthew was still smiling, but his smile had grown uncertain. His vulnerability moved her, a shiver along the spine that resembled love.

"Some mistakes are too big to undo," he said. "Mori's not me anymore, but he's going to follow me to the grave."

She wanted to reassure him, but didn't know how. What could she say? That she didn't mind? She *did* mind. It wasn't that she'd hadn't had lovers with tattoos. One man had been literally covered with them, his entire body from wrists to ankles a canvas filled with runes, dragons, angels, and ideograms. But this was different. The skeleton was a shadow that wavered between them.

"I can put my shirt back on."

"No, don't."

Mar leaned down, her face near Matthew's chest. The skull grinned at her. Didn't all skulls grin? A terrible smile lay under the surface of every living face.

She touched her lips to the skull's lips. They were warm, which surprised her: she'd half expected a rigor-mortis chill. Then she kissed one of Matthew's nipples, which hardened, alive, under her tongue. He groaned and pulled her head close. He was sweating slightly. She inhaled the sweet musk of his skin.

Because Matthew was coming in from Mt. Hope that afternoon, a Sunday, she called to cancel the evening's supper with Pearl.

"Sorry," she said, realizing as she spoke that she hadn't

invented a good lie. "There's a project, a deadline. It came up at the last minute. I have to work here at home."

Pearl was silent. Through the receiver Mar heard a car alarm go off. "Young people always got something important to do."

The retort made Mar's face tighten with shame.

"Too bad 'cause I made *siu mai*. Your favorite."

She could see Pearl wheeling her shopping cart in the early morning cold, a silk scarf knotted under her chin, the fingertips of her Isotoner gloves worn thin with use. She saw her picking over the mustard greens for the freshest bunch, haggling with the shopkeeper in loud Cantonese. The shrimp for the *siu mai* glistened like gray-green shards of sea glass. She saw Pearl bump the heavy cart back up the six flights of stairs. Perhaps she treated herself to a forbidden second cup of coffee before settling in to the work of chopping and washing and measuring out the rice.

She should have let Pearl know on Saturday, right after Matthew called, but she'd waited till now, as if avoidance alone might solve the problem. It had been easier to tell Curt, her trader, that Thursdays were off due to a family emergency and that she'd call him at work when she could. Like Pearl, he heard the lie in her voice, but unlike Pearl he accepted it. A few weeks earlier he'd told Mar that his wife was starting to suspect. Not exactly suspect, he said, but she knows something, she feels it, the way you feel uneasy in your bones just before you come down with the flu.

"Next Sunday, come uptown. It'll be my treat," Mar said into the receiver.

Pearl didn't speak for several long seconds. "You're pretty smart, but you spend too much money," she finally said. "You should cook more, like I been trying to teach you."

"It's just that I'm so busy."

"Always busy."

"Sorry."

"Go work," Pearl said.

Mar set the bottle of red wine on the table next to the roses she'd bought an hour earlier at the Indian grocery on the corner. The excitement she felt about seeing Matthew was now clouded with guilt. She had handled things badly, had hurt Pearl. Perhaps her cruelty would curse them. In the bedroom, which was right next to the kitchen, she shook out fresh sheets—the ones with the embroidered flowers she'd found at the Goodwill—and thought of Matthew's callused hands, the roughness against her skin. His eyes. The smiling skull. Before she could stop it, the thought surfaced that one day she would hurt him so badly he'd never want to speak her name again.

When it happened, Mar was on her hands and knees with Matthew kneeling behind her, gripping her hips. The steam heat was up high. They were both sweating. It seemed as though they had been in bed forever, making love, talking, and making love again. Whipped by a breeze from the open window, the burned-down candles guttered and roared.

"Don't stop," Mar groaned.

A slight trembling passed from Matthew's body into hers. "Quiet," he whispered.

The dead bolt opened with a shot. Mar's door swung open a crack, stopped short by the chain.

"Margaret?"

A blade of light from the hall slashed the kitchen floor. The voice belonged to Pearl. Mar felt Matthew relax. The intruder was a woman, just a woman, no real threat. The door strained against the chain. She could guess what Pearl saw: the dark apartment, flickering candles, Matthew's shirt hanging over the back of a kitchen chair. Could she hear their breath? Smell the sweat and wine?

Minutes seemed to pass. Mar's legs quivered with the effort of holding still.

"I know you're busy," Pearl said coldly. "I'm leaving the food you didn't come eat. It's in the hall."

The door slammed shut. Matthew moved away from her, then lay down on his side. Still trembling, Mar listened to the shopping cart clang down the stairs. Only when she couldn't hear it anymore did she lean over to switch on the lamp.

"Who in the world was that?"

She thought he would be angry, but his expression was neutral. Getting up, she went into the kitchen and slid his shirt over her shoulders. On the doormat were two red plastic shopping bags stretched tight with ricotta containers. She blew out the candles, then set the bags on the table. Wrapped in a paper towel bordered with blue geese and hearts was a single pair of wooden chopsticks. Despite herself, she smiled. Pearl didn't trust her to have her own.

"Why aren't you telling me who it was?"

Instead of answering, she lay down on the bed, her head against his hip. Pearl would be halfway to Second Avenue by now, her eyes tearing from the cold. What time was it, nine or ten? She couldn't imagine Pearl out so late. Desperate to get the image of the old woman and her empty cart out of her mind, she turned and slipped Matthew's penis into her mouth. When he reached for a new condom, she stopped him. Moaning, he laced his hands into her hair. The skeleton's pelvis arched inches from her nose.

When they were done, Matthew lay on his back, staring at the ceiling. She wondered if he was looking at the shadow of the ceiling fan, a tremendous dark flower blossoming on the pressed tin. His expression was thoughtful. Worried.

"You didn't have to do that," he said. "You can trust me, but how do *you* know? It's not like we've known each other all our lives."

"Didn't you like it?"

"That's not the point."

She got up, went into the kitchen, and came back with Pearl's bags. She also brought an extra set of chopsticks, and, just in case, a fork.

"You still haven't told me who she was."

"My great-aunt."

Matthew picked up his chopsticks. "Are you two close?"

Mar shook her head no. She couldn't even begin to explain.

"OK, we don't have to talk about it."

While they ate, they spoke about small heartbreaks and work. She was relieved that Matthew did most of the talking. Before computer programming, he'd been an EMT, which he loved because instead of just standing around in a crisis he could actually do something. Gradually, the doubt that clouded his face disappeared. He appeared to have decided something. He would leave her, she knew. She wondered if after that night she would ever see him again.

∽

When the police called, she was deep within a dream about her grandfather, who smiled down at her from his big blue armchair. The insides of his nostrils were dark caves. Because of the perspective, she realized she was a small child.

"What should I do?" she asked.

His eyes said, *You know what to do.*

An alarm began to howl. The world outside her grandparents' house was orange with flames. Fire caressed the pine trees and hydrangeas, which pulsated in the heat as if moved by a giant's breath.

The telephone was ringing. She tried to get out of bed, but something stopped her—arms wrapped around her, a man's warm arms. Before she could pull herself free, the answering machine came on. Her own voice filled the room, reciting her number and asking the caller to leave a brief message after the tone.

"What? What is it?" Matthew mumbled. She clicked on the reading lamp. Glancing at his chest, she felt her throat tighten, but the darkness wasn't a terrible burn called down by her dream, it was only his tattoo.

She picked up the receiver. The glowing numbers on the clock radio read 2:07. Without having to be told, she knew someone had died.

"Who is it?"

"Margaret Lau?" The voice was a woman's.

"I'm Margaret Lau."

"Officer E. P. Morales with the Ninth Precinct. Are you related to a Mrs. Jee-you Lau?"

"No. I mean, yes." *Jyu.* Pearl. It was Pearl.

"The situation's under control."

"What situation?"

Matthew looked up at her questioningly. She shook

her head and continued listening to Officer Morales's uninflected monotone. At around 9 p.m. that evening, Mrs. Lau experienced a fall on Second Avenue, near the corner of Seventh Street. She was taken, with head injuries and injuries to her left arm, to Bellevue Hospital Emergency Room, where she was now.

"Is she alive?"

"Her condition's stable."

"She's OK?"

"She's stable. The attending physician, a Dr. Stillman, can tell you more. Would you like the number?"

"What happened?"

"She experienced a fall."

"No, I mean what *happened?*"

Officer Morales paused. Mar could hear the rustle of paper. "She wasn't accosted or anything like that. Witnesses said she just fell."

Matthew's hands rested on her shoulders. Instead of shaking him off, she leaned into them. It was then that she realized she was trembling.

"How did you find me?" she said. "Did Pearl, Mrs. Lau . . ."

"Mrs. Lau was conscious but incoherent. Her address book was in her purse."

"And you called me?"

"You were the only Lau listed. The only Lau with a local address and phone number."

Her throat tingled. She took a deep breath. *The only Lau.* Pearl needed her. "Wait," she said, "I've got to find a pen."

"What's going on?" Matthew asked, after she put down the phone. He leaned back against her pillows. A few minutes ago she'd been asleep in his arms. She had never slept that deeply in someone's arms before, not since unremembered infancy.

"My aunt," she said.

"The mystery aunt with the food?"

Quickly, she told him what she knew. She then punched in the number she'd written on a paper napkin, was transferred, and put on hold. Long seconds later, a woman with the same flat voice as Officer Morales said there was no one by the name of Jyu Lau or Pearl Lau currently admitted to the ER.

"Please look again."

The woman sighed. Mar gathered her clothes from the floor.

"Still no Jyu or Pearl Lau."

Matthew was telling her something. "Try another spelling," he mouthed.

"What about L A N? L A W? L A M? L O W?" she said, racing through the usual ways her name, their name, was mangled by the people Pearl called Americans.

"I already tried. Nothing."

Mar glanced down at the crumpled napkin. "Dr. Stillman. Can you get me through to Dr. Stillman?"

"Stillman." She heard the soft click-click of computer keys. "Dr. Stillman's currently on duty. He'll have to call you back."

"When?"

"When he can."

She was finished dressing before she noticed Matthew had gotten into his clothes, too.

"I'm going with you." When she hesitated, he said, "Though she doesn't know it, I was your Aunt Pearl's guest for dinner. You could say I owe her."

She hunted for her bag. The light irony of his remark

sank deep. Didn't she owe Pearl? Pearl had given her family. The immensity of her debt stunned her.

"Let's hurry," she said.

Plastic orange seats filled the waiting room. A Chinese family took up most of the front row, but otherwise the place was empty.

The white-tiled floor was gray with a patina of grime. Mar crossed it to the wall of glass where a woman sat behind a half-moon hole. When the woman looked up, Mar saw that the heavy gold bands in her ears stretched the lobes down like Buddha's. The light from the computer screen tinted her dark face blue. "Nope," she said. "No Laus."

"Please keep looking. I'm sure she's here," Mar said, although she wasn't sure at all.

While the woman typed, Mar stared down at her desk, on which lay a Magic Marker, a Lotto ticket, and an egg-salad sandwich sliced in half, the thin wax paper that enfolded it sliced in half, too. The fluorescent light buzzed. The sandwich had one or two bites taken out of it; a few tiny cubes of egg white had fallen onto the foil below. For some reason, the sight saddened her even more than the institutional stink of wet wool and disinfectant. How lost you could become in this city. How easy it was to wait in waiting rooms like this, to sit in your apartment, to walk down the street, to eat and live and die, and all the while not be seen. Old women were the most easily lost, and now Pearl was among the lost. Even her name was lost.

"J Y U, right?" The woman hit a key, and the printer started to hum. "Female, head injuries, possible heart. Approximately eighty years of age."

"That's her." Was Pearl eighty? Her skin looked so smooth.

The woman slid a yellow sheet of paper through the hole in the glass. "This is your pass." Without looking up at it, she pointed to the clock on the waiting-room wall. "On the hour you can go in for fifteen minutes, fifteen minutes only. On the hour means on the hour. You'll have to wait."

Mar took the sheet, which was still warm from the printer. "What does 'possible heart' mean?"

But the woman had already turned away. If she had heard, she wasn't going to answer.

Mar sat on one of the orange chairs right behind the Chinese family. They were Fujianese, she decided, the loudness with which they spoke a dead giveaway. One woman was using chopsticks to feed a child from a quart-sized container of soup noodles. He opened his mouth but didn't look at the woman, his mother or aunt, who was scooping out noodles so neatly not a drop of liquid flecked his blue-and-white-striped Yankees pajama top.

Matthew was talking to the uniformed guard at the entrance to the Emergency Room. When he saw that she was looking, he waved her over.

"We can go in now," he said.

It was 2:46. Mar looked questioningly at the guard, who nodded yes.

In the corridor behind the swinging doors was a metal gurney, on which lay a Latino man in his early twenties. One leg of his jeans had been cut off. The wide white bandage that covered his thigh was bright with blood. A young woman with darkly painted lips leaned over him, reading aloud from the paper—a *News* or a *Post*—spread open on his chest to a photograph of Monica Lewinsky standing before a car on a suburban-looking street.

Beyond lay a vast white room. Gurneys and hospital beds angled from the walls like parallel-parked cars. The disinfectant smell grew stronger, almost masking the metallic scent of blood.

Matthew squeezed her hand. "The first lesson I learned as an EMT is things usually aren't as bad as they seem."

He steered her into the glare. Machines rhythmically beeped. Someone was groaning. Alone in a glassed-off room lay a man whose face was so obscured by dirt she couldn't determine his race. His eyes were closed. He didn't move.

They had reached the nurses' island. A man in a green surgical blouse with smudged wire-rim glasses glanced up from his stack of papers. He seemed no older than twenty-four or -five.

"We're trying to find Mrs. Jyu Lau," said Matthew.

Mar scanned the rows of beds and gurneys, afraid to look too closely at the twisted or still bodies. On a bed just a few steps away, she saw a shock of luxuriant white hair. It was Pearl. One whole side of her face was purple and yellow. Mar took a breath, walked closer. The face looked painted: inhuman, brutal, brutalized.

"Pearl?"

Both eyes were closed. The injured eye was swollen tight as a plum. Without wanting to, Mar noticed that it looked like the glans of a penis. She touched a hand, the one without the IV. The thin flesh dappled with age spots felt dry and cool.

"Can you hear me, Pearl?"

Pearl's hospital gown was open, the sheet pulled up to

cover her breasts. The skin was soft looking, as if her body was decades younger than the bizarre face above. Stuck to her chest were several round white patches with wires that ran to a monitor. On the TV mounted near the ceiling, like the TVs in motels, two lines traced sinuous blue and green waves.

Eyes still closed, Pearl softly moaned. The lines on the TV screen stopped moving. The word APNEA flashed in red.

Mar felt the blood drain from her face. Without knowing how she got there, she was standing again at the nurses' island, where Matthew and the man in green still talked.

"I think something's wrong." Her voice sounded too quiet. "What's 'apnea' mean? It's happening to Pearl."

The man smiled up at Mar. "I'm Dr. Stillman," he said. "You're the niece?"

Numbly, she nodded.

"We're keeping a good eye on her. That's why her bed is so close to the station."

Mar glanced back at Pearl's TV screen, which was again filled with sea-colored waves. Dr. Stillman was saying that Pearl had a concussion and a hairline fracture. "We're watching her heart. It's highly possible she fell because she passed out."

"What's apnea?" Mar asked again.

Dr. Stillman took off his glasses, wiped them on the edge of his blouse. "Literally, it means 'cessation.' For a moment, her heart ceases to beat. Know how long she's had this condition?"

Mar waited to be told. Then, realizing that he was waiting for an answer, she said, "I don't."

Suddenly Dr. Stillman looked very tired. "OK, we'll

run more tests, another EKG. There should be more news in the morning."

"Can I stay with her?"

"Sure," he said. "It's a good idea. When she wakes up, she'll be pretty disoriented."

Mar walked back over to Pearl. Through the veil of noise she heard Matthew dictate her phone number to Dr. Stillman. He already had it memorized, then. Briefly moved by this evidence of his attention, she gazed at Pearl's monitor. *The niece.* She'd never thought of herself as a real niece, but to a doctor or other stranger, she must appear like a niece in a normal family that gathered together for Christmas or New Year's or whatever rituals they happened to share. If she saw herself as strangers did, she could be anything she wanted, anything at all.

A streak of dried blood arched over Pearl's wounded eye like a second eyebrow. How she would hate knowing every beat and tremor of her heart was on display for all to see. *We're watching her heart.* Had anyone, even Third Uncle, ever watched her so closely? Mar was gripped by the urge to paint a portrait of Pearl, wounded and revealed. Some niece she was. She was as good as an outsider, a stranger looking in at a stranger's life. A voyeur, nothing more.

Matthew gave her one of the two paper cups of water he held. By the clock on the pillar that rose from the middle of the nurses' island, it was 4:20.

"You don't have to stay."

"I know."

The rhythmic beep that marked each beat of Pearl's heart grew faster. She stirred. The good eye opened. Startled, Mar put down the undrunk water and took her hand. Part of her had expected Pearl to go on sleeping forever.

"Pearl?"

The limp fingers twitched.

"Pearl?"

"I heard you the first time." Her voice sounded scratchy, as if she hadn't spoken in a year. The eye squinted at Mar, then roved around the room, taking in Matthew, the clock, the blue curtains that hung between beds, the orderly wheeling an empty gurney through the swinging doors.

"Where am I?"

Mar took a breath. "The hospital. You had a fall."

"Where did I fall?"

"Second Avenue."

"What was I doing on Second Avenue?"

Mar glanced at Matthew, who nodded, then left. Another orderly, dredlocks tucked under his scrub cap, wheeled a hospital bed, on which lay an ancient white woman, into the space next to Pearl.

"Where am I?" Pearl said.

"The hospital."

Smiling, Mar stroked Pearl's hand. Inside, she burned with grief and guilt. Pearl's memory was gone. The memories that made her who she was were gone, and it was all her fault.

"You the doctor? You don't look like no doctor to me."

The eye focused now on Matthew, who had returned with Dr. Stillman. "You don't look like doctors neither."

"I'm a resident," Dr. Stillman said gently.

"A resident of where?"

"Dr. Morse is here to examine you."

A large woman in her forties, wearing a white doctor's coat, stepped into the small enclosure, then pulled the curtain closed around them. Her blond hair was held in place by two barrettes shaped like musical notes. She looked like someone who, in her non-emergency-room life, knew how to enjoy herself.

"Hello, Mrs. Lau." Her cheerfulness was neither forced nor completely natural. Lowering her voice, she said, to Mar, "Does she speak English?"

"Yes."

"How are you feeling, Mrs. Lau?"

Pearl opened her eye a little wider. "I been better."

"I'm going to ask you a few questions, OK?"

Almost imperceptibly, Pearl nodded.

"Who's the president, Mrs. Lau?"

"I don't pay no attention to those politicians." She winced—or was it a grin?—then gave a small, dry cough.

"Give you a hint. He's sleeping with someone he shouldn't be."

"Gossip. I don't listen." Pearl's voice grew louder, warming. "They all sleep with someone. What's so new about that?"

Dr. Morse smiled broadly. "Bill Clinton," she said. "Good old William Jefferson Clinton. He's our president. OK, here's the next question. What month is it?"

"Why do you want to know?"

"Humor me. What month is it?"

Pearl gazed at her blankly, then tucked her chin slightly so as to stare at the laminated ID tag that hung by a chain around Dr. Morse's neck.

"Here's another hint. Thanksgiving comes this month."

"What's there to be thankful for? November. It's November."

"And who's the president?"

Pearl paused. "Clinton."

Dr. Morse seemed to relax, as if she'd been holding her breath. "Very good. Bill Clinton, that's right."

"He doesn't know how to keep his you-know-what in his pants. None of them do."

The doctor laughed, a real laugh this time. Her teeth were slightly yellow at the roots. She looked at Mar and said, "That's a good sign." Then, to Pearl, she said, more loudly, "We'll see what's going on with your heart and get you out of here as soon as we can."

"Good, 'cause I want to go home. No reason to keep me in this cage."

Pearl seemed to deflate again. She looked old and terribly wounded. Dr. Morse glanced meaningfully at Mar and Matthew. "Don't worry, Mrs. Lau, we're doing our best."

The ancient woman next to Pearl was fast asleep. Her eyelids were partly open; two white crescents glowed beneath the white lashes. The clock on the pillar read 5:51. A rainbow haze, the radiance of exhaustion, pulsed around its face. Although she wanted to eat some diner eggs and fall asleep, Mar couldn't leave until Pearl came back to herself.

She took a sip of water, then set the cup back down on the table. Pearl stirred as if out of a dream. "Where am I?"

"The hospital."

Mar took her hand and squeezed it, more firmly than she'd intended.

"How did I get here?"

"You fell."

"Where did I fall?"

The screen above Pearl's head flashed red. *Apnea. Cessation.* A little death. The nurse or doctor or resident who sat in the chair vacated by Dr. Stillman didn't even look up from the pile of papers she was poring over.

"Listen," Mar said, "do you remember coming to see me last night?"

Doubt clouded Pearl's eye.

"Do you know who I am?"

"Don't," Matthew murmured.

"Who am I?" Mar said. She couldn't rest until Pearl answered. She needed the woman who had miraculously identified her to once again know who she was.

Pearl stared up at her suspiciously. "You're the doctor who's keeping me in this cage." Her beautiful white hair flowed over the pillow. Her one open eye went dark, focused inward. "It hurts," she said. "You're the doctor, so do something."

"I'm sorry. I'm sorry it hurts."

"I'll go find an ice pack." Matthew lowered his voice. "After that, we'll leave. She'll recognize you when she's ready, Margaret. Your aunt needs to rest."

Mar gazed at Pearl's bruised face, then touched her own, surprised to feel it wet with tears. After a few minutes, Matthew returned. He wrapped the ice pack in a small white towel and laid it gently against the swollen brow.

"Hold it with this hand. That's right." He adjusted the pillow under Pearl. "We're going to go soon. Is there anything else you need?"

"Don't."

"Don't what?"

"Don't go. What kind of doctors are you?"

Mar leaned down, kissed the uninjured cheek. "We'll stay a little while longer, OK?"

Pearl's eye gleamed with cautious trust. At 6:29, she nodded off and began to snore. The green and blue waves beat to a quieter rhythm. Feeling as if she was committing a minor crime, Mar walked with Matthew toward the swinging doors. In the glassed-in room near the entrance lay a sheet-wrapped figure curled in a fetal tuck. Was it the same man, masked with grime, she had glimpsed nearly four hours before? Mar had never seen a human being lie so still. Stillness seemed to emanate from the body, and it was by this she knew that the person swaddled in the sheet was dead.

Steam trapped behind the clear curtain around the bathtub blurred Matthew's body. All she could distinctly see was the flash of an arm or thigh, the darkness of his hair. Stretching the coiled wire taut, she walked the phone into the bedroom so her mother wouldn't hear the sound of the shower. Matthew's shirt and jeans lay on the unmade bed, accidentally arranged so that they looked inhabited by a fleshless body. It seemed impossible that only a few hours ago they had made love.

"So you've taken up with Pearl," Mar's mother was saying. "I'm not surprised."

Mar twisted the cord around her wrist.

"When she wants to, she can be very charming."

Charming wasn't a word Mar could connect to the old woman lying in Bellevue. When she didn't speak, her mother said, "You're a good girl to look after her."

"I am?"

Paper crackled. "I think her daughter lives in Tampa or Ft. Lauderdale. Here, I found it. Tampa."

Surprised that her mother actually possessed Pearl's daughter's address, Mar said, "When's the last time you wrote?"

"Christmas. You know, Christmas cards. Dolores always sends one with a picture of cats."

Until she was a teenager old enough to object, Mar's

family's cards were made from photographs of Mar standing before the last year's tinseled tree. Had Pearl seen one of those cards? Perhaps Pearl was on the Christmas list. Maybe the extended family Mar had imagined as completely scattered was actually held together by ties that shriveled but didn't break, like the sinews on unclean skeletons that cleave hard to the bone.

"No phone number. I'll have to call information." Her mother paused. "You OK, sweetie? I imagine Bellevue was no picnic."

"I'm fine."

"Dad and I will be there as soon as we can."

The water stopped running. Matthew parted the shower curtain, releasing a cloud of steam.

"Mom?"

"What, honey?"

"How many oranges are lucky?"

Her mother laughed. "What are you talking about?"

"You know, the oranges you give people. When you go to visit." Twisting the cord tighter, Mar waited for the answer.

After she hung up, she pushed Matthew's clothes to one side, lay down, and watched him dry himself off. When he rubbed the towel over his chest, she half expected the tattoo to smear, but, of course, his skeleton was indelible, etched into his skin. She thought of Pearl's white bosom pocked with electrodes. Mar herself had been wiped clean from Pearl's memory. If she did exist, it was in an unreadable form, like graffiti bleeding through a covering coat of paint.

Matthew hung the towel back on the hook, then walked over to the bed. She liked the muscled hollows of his hips. His stomach was a little soft, which she found sweet. He was becoming familiar. Even Memento Mori wasn't so strange.

She made room for him to lie down. Still fully clothed, she rested her head against his chest. During the cab ride back to her apartment, she'd thought he would want to flee—she would, if the roles were reversed—but he seemed happier than ever to be with her.

"You're pretty close to your mystery aunt," he said now.

"You think?"

"And she's close to you."

With one finger, Mar traced the skeleton's jutting knee. "She's forgotten me, or didn't you notice?"

"No, she hasn't. She was just disoriented. Short-term memory loss is pretty common in these cases. It's all waiting just beneath the surface, though."

"All?"

"All except the last half hour or so before the trauma. Usually, that's impossible to retrieve."

Mar felt a small flare of relief. Maybe the shame between them would be erased. Maybe Pearl wouldn't remember how, driven by the loneliness she'd never admit, she had walked through the night, in the cold, only to be locked out, betrayed for the man who lay here now.

Making love again would be the appropriate thing to do, but Mar was so tired. In an hour, she would have to call in sick to work.

Matthew's eyes were closed. One lid twitched. "Let's get unconscious ourselves. Sleep," he whispered.

His heart lifted her head slightly with each beat, the gentlest rocking she had ever known.

The glass room that held the corpse was now empty. Even the bed was gone.

A few drops of water dripped from the tip of the paper

cone that held the roses. She laid the flowers on the table that, supported by a single arm, hovered over the foot of Pearl's bed. Pearl was asleep. Sometime during the night, the ancient woman who shared her enclosure had been removed. In her place was another elderly white woman, who beamed at Mar.

"This is Edna, dearie," said the Black woman standing between the beds. "Edna loves it when you say her name. Isn't that right, Edna?"

The old woman laughed a breathy huh, huh, huh.

"She fell." The home-care nurse spoke with a Caribbean accent, soothing and slow. "I thought it best to take her here, just in case."

"Hi, Edna," Mar said. Looking more closely, she saw that the patient wasn't as old as she'd first believed. She seemed to be in her late fifties or early sixties.

"Early-onset Alzheimer's," the nurse said. "Edna loves hearing her name because it's one of the few things she still remembers."

Slightly shaken, Mar turned back to Pearl. The bruised half of her face was almost completely purple now, the dark purple of rotten fruit. The crust of blood over her eye was gone.

"I need something to put these roses in. Any ideas?" Mar asked.

"Try down there, dearie."

In the cabinet next to the sink was a curved plastic container shaped like a gourd. When she saw it, the nurse chuckled.

"That's a portable urinal. Men got it easier than we do. All they have to do is stick it in."

Mar ran a stream of water into the wide mouth. The roses protruded at an angle. She set them, along with the five oranges she'd brought, on the table. Positioning the table's arm so that her offering would be the first thing Pearl saw, she considered the question of blame. If she really was the good girl her mother said she was and had gone to Pearl's for Sunday supper, none of this would have happened. If only she had been kinder, or at least more careful. But wasn't Pearl responsible, too? If Pearl had stayed where she was supposed to, in Chinatown, and not gone on her furious mission of mercy or revenge, Mar wouldn't be standing over her arranging flowers in a plastic urinal.

"I'm here," she said softly. "I brought you roses, your favorite."

Coughing, Pearl opened her good eye. Mar found a plastic cup, which she filled with water. When Pearl looked at the cup but didn't raise her hands, Mar held it to her lips.

"Do you know who I am?"

Water streamed down Pearl's neck. "You think I'm that far gone? You're Robert's daughter." She pushed the cup away. "I'm so tired. The noise all night long, like Grand Central Station."

"Do you know why you're here?"

"What is this, twenty questions? I fell. People fall. Now I want to go home. Morty needs me."

Edna's nurse gave Mar a surreptitious smile. "Upsy-daisy, old girl," she said. "Let's sit you up a little."

"You can't, not yet. They have to run more tests," Mar said.

"Always more tests. What do they think they'll find? Gold?" The scowl faded. "Morty's all alone. He's only three years old in human years. Just a baby."

"I'll take care of him."

"He's hungry."

"So I'll feed him."

"He needs *me* to feed him."

"You can't, not yet."

"I know. The tests."

Pearl looked sternly up at Mar. "He only eats noodles and jelly beans. Be sure not to give him the licorice. He hates the licorice ones. Promise you won't forget."

"I promise." Mar stroked Pearl's hand, a caress she endured.

"Promise this, too. That you won't tell my daughter."

Mar paused. Technically, it was a promise she could keep. As far as she knew, Pearl's daughter had already been called, and her mother, not Mar, had done the calling.

"Swear." Pearl lifted her head a feather's width off the pillow, her eyes wide with pleading, an expression Mar had never seen in them before.

"I swear I won't tell."

Pearl relaxed back into the bed. "Good," she said, "'cause I hate Florida. It's a boneyard. A boneyard full of sun."

Her one open eye clouded over with exhaustion and closed. Soon, she was snoring.

When she woke again, a few minutes later, her bad eye opened a crack, too. The white was streaked bright red, the color of just-spilled blood.

"What's that there on the table?"

"Roses." Mar lifted an orange from the plastic bag. "I brought these, too."

Pearl shook her head. "Never did like them."

"I brought five of them."

"Good for you."

Stung, Mar tried to keep her smile steady. "Should I offer one to your neighbor?"

"Who?"

Mar turned to the home-care nurse. "Do you want an orange? Does she?"

"Thanks, dearie."

The scent of oranges filled the curtained enclosure. The nurse carefully peeled the membrane off a section, then nudged it into her charge's mouth. "Chew, Edna. Yum, yum, yum. That's right. They forget how to chew," she said to Mar. "They forget how to swallow. After that, it doesn't take long."

With a folded paper towel, the nurse wiped the orange flesh from Edna's chin. Mar felt her heart constrict.

"You know I love you," she said to Pearl.

Instantly she felt uneasy, as if the act of uttering the words made her suspect their truth.

Pearl closed her eyes. She didn't smile, but her battered face was suffused with an expression that might have been joy. She kept her eyes closed until Dr. Morse walked up to the bed and asked how she was feeling that day.

"Do you know who I am?"

Pearl snapped to attention. "Why does everyone want me to tell them who they are? You're the lady who wants to know about the president."

"That's right, you got my number."

"All men are rotten eggs. It's only a matter of time."

Dr. Morse looked up at the monitor, studying it intently. "Let's get the question of that heart murmur settled once and for all." She tugged at one of the wires. The white circle of tape holding it to Pearl's chest came loose, leaving a red circle on the skin.

"What are you doing?" Pearl's eyes were glazed with fear.

"We're taking you over to radiology, Mrs. Lau."

"More tests?"

"More tests."

Pearl tried to lift herself up on her hands, and, failing, slumped back into the bed. "I'll go, but only if you make her promise not to tell my daughter."

Dr. Morse smiled tiredly at Mar. "Don't you want your daughter to know?"

"I hate Florida."

"It's OK," Mar said. "I promise."

"Make her swear."

"I swear."

"This is going to take awhile," Dr. Morse said to Mar. "After we're done, we're going to transfer her to the Cardiac ICU. You might as well go home."

Watching the orderly wheel Pearl through the double doors, Mar was filled with guilty relief. She had been told to leave—told to disappear from this fluorescent hell with its stink of old food, ammonia, urine, and fear—and so she had no choice. She was absolved of responsibility.

A world away from the rush-hour noise outside, Pearl's kitchen was washed in silent darkness. Waving her hand, Mar found the light string hanging from the ceiling. In the glare that was both too bright and too dim, the room, bereft of Pearl's presence, looked like the den of someone who'd gone mad.

The stovetop and lip of the porcelain sink were spattered with teardrops of grease. In the sink lay two frying pans and a tower of steamers. A large cockroach balanced on the tines of a dirty fork, its antennae delicately feeling the air.

Mar shooed it away, then turned on the water. The Handi Wipe folded over the faucet was gray with use and age. Finished, she dried her hands on her sweater, scrutinizing the vials of drugs on the table. Nitroglycerin, Lasix. Chinese pills in thick brown bottles. A few English words stood out among the ideograms. *Eight lozenges day and night. Indications for the liver.*

Slowly, she walked to the front of the apartment, turning on lights, wondering what secrets might be laid bare without Pearl to guard them. Above the unused bed, Pearl's younger self stared off into the distance. Although she smiled, her eyes were blank.

Morty hung by his claws from the side of the cage. Turning his head, he bit one bar, beak parted to reveal a gray-black tongue.

"Do you know who I am, birdie?" Mar asked.

His eyes were glowing beads. She opened the cage door, then cautiously stuck in a finger the way Pearl did when inviting him to come to her.

Morty leapt from the cage onto his perch. The pain was so sharp her eyes teared. Blood welled from the gash just below her cuticle. Cupping her other hand underneath to catch the blood, Mar strode back into the kitchen. Red drops splashed into the sink, blending with the stains she'd been unable to scrub clean.

When the bleeding slowed, she saw that the wound was small but deep. In the crowded medicine cabinet, she hunted without luck for Band-Aids. The closest she came was a box of corn pads, the same adhesive circles her grandfather wore on his toes. She'd thought only women used them because of their high heels. When she had asked her mother, she'd said, "His feet hurt because he stands all the time. People who work in restaurants have to stand."

Although his door stood open, Morty hadn't moved

from his perch. Glancing at his water, which fed into the cage through a small tube, Mar saw it was almost full. She opened the wings of the container of lo mein she had picked up on the way over, then set it on the TV tray. If he got hungry enough, he'd find it.

She paused before the ancestor shrine. The once-terrifying great-grandfather solemnly regarded her. While Morty frantically skittered back and forth, Mar lifted the portrait from its place. Pearl's photograph was harder to reach. She had to push aside two piles of blouses to make enough room on the bed to stand. The bedsprings screeched. A film of greasy dust coated the glass. She took the frame off its hook, leaving behind a clean rectangle on the wall.

Before she had time to wonder at the mild insanity of her act, she was back in the kitchen. The plastic bag on the top of the stack had been smoothed out so not a wrinkle remained. She shook it open and slipped the portraits inside.

When she turned the key in the dead-bolt lock, the bitten finger started to bleed again. A few drops of blood dripped onto the plastic that sheathed Pearl and her great-grandfather. Mar shook the blood off, locked the final lock, and started down the stairs.

The curtains that hung from the ceiling of the Coronary ICU rippled in the air whispering from the vents. At that hour, the unit was dimly lit and quiet—as dim and quiet as the ER had been loud. The only real sound was the underwater ping of the monitors.

Behind one curtain lay a sleeping Black man with ashen, puffy cheeks. Behind another was a white man whose mouth stretched wide around an accordioned hose. A machine hissed, and his chest rose, filling with mechanical breath. His eyes were slightly open, but Mar understood that he, too, was unconscious or asleep.

Pearl was behind the next curtain, her bed cranked up so she could sit. Green light playing over her face, she gazed up at something Mar couldn't see. The bruise was now so dark it looked black.

"How are you feeling?" Mar bent down to kiss the unbruised cheek.

Pearl glanced at her, then stared back upward. Following the path of her gaze, Mar saw a TV mounted near the ceiling. Football players crouched on a jewel green field, frozen between plays.

"I know who you are." Pearl's voice was faint and hoarse. "You took my blood a minute ago. Don't you got enough?"

Eyes still fixed on the TV, she coughed, then reached for the paper cup on the table.

"Here, let me get that for you." Mar felt a spasm of dismay. Pearl had forgotten her again. Either that or she magically sensed what Mar had stolen. *Borrowed*, she said to herself, because she resolved to return the portraits the following day. She had carefully cleaned the glass that protected Pearl's face. A decades-old water stain spread a lacy fan over the left-hand corner of the matting. The photo's emulsion had started to fade, tinting Pearl's skin and dress a delicate brown. Time had intruded, after all. Propped against a box in Mar's apartment, the picture seemed strangely ordinary, the halo of mystery around it gone.

Something moved at the periphery of her vision, and

it was then Mar realized they weren't alone. A woman wearing a sweater with black-and-white patches shaped like diamonds leaned against the radiator casing, her arms crossed over her chest. She stared at Mar.

Mar nodded hello. "Dolores? How was your flight?"

The woman blinked. A pair of glasses with red plastic frames hung from a chain around her neck.

"Fine."

She was in her forties—no, fifties—and she possessed Pearl's long straight nose and oval face. But this woman, her second cousin, was not beautiful. Gray strands like steel shavings curled from her short black hair. She looked like Pearl, but entirely without the queenly beauty.

On the sole chair were two plastic bags bulging with fruit and takeout containers. Dolores waved vaguely around the room, a gesture taking in the tremendous floral arrangement that had replaced Mar's roses. "Have a seat," she said.

The bed next to Pearl's was empty. Mar had to hop up to reach the mattress. Her legs dangled without touching the floor.

"I think you've got something of my mother's. Her keys," Dolores said.

Pearl stared up at the game, green and white light flickering in her eyes.

Mar said, "It's me, Pearl. Robert's daughter, Margaret. You know me. When I was this big, you held me in your arms."

"The keys," Dolores said.

Mar's cheeks burned. She'd never felt such cold hatred aimed her way. She slid down from the high bed. After fumbling for a long minute or two, she managed to detach Pearl's keys from her chain. "Here you go," she said. When

Pearl made no move to accept them, she laid the keys on the table.

"Your parents are downstairs," Dolores said. "I think they went to the cafeteria."

"I guess I'll go find them, then."

When Mar leaned over to kiss her, Pearl almost imperceptibly flinched. Mar looked at her searchingly, but her great-aunt gazed straight ahead.

She found her mother seated at a table in the lobby. The snack bar was closed, the lights above turned off, leaving her in semidarkness. Before her was a Styrofoam cup of coffee stained red at the rim.

"There you are, dear."

Mar embraced her. Her mother looked tired, the bags under her eyes deeper than they were the last time. She wondered what her mother saw and didn't say about her. Too thin, too pale. Too far from innocence.

"Where's Dad?"

"Out walking off some steam." Her mother's eyes brightened with mirth. "Have you been up to see them? In the tiger's den?"

Trying to hide her answering smile, Mar sat down beside her. Bathed in her mother's presence, she felt better, the tears of angry shame on the elevator ride down already half forgotten.

"Dolores thinks there's a conspiracy afoot. I'm afraid she blames you." Her mother blotted her mouth on a paper napkin, leaving a faint, rosy kiss. "Don't let them bother you. Pearl's always been that way."

"What way?"

"And Dolores is cut from the same cloth. I could see it the minute I walked into the room."

She folded the napkin, then tucked it into her purse. "It was nice of you to be kind to old Pearl. Like I said, you're a good girl."

The man walking toward them, shoes resounding on the marble floor, was her father. He smiled when he saw her, gave her a quick kiss. His face, red from the cold, smelled of cigarette smoke. In the bag he carried were two sandwiches in white paper. Her mother unwrapped the one marked with a T.

"It's turkey. Take half," she said to Mar.

Shreds of iceberg lettuce, pale confetti, lay scattered on the wax paper. They ate quietly. Mar's parents would be taking the 9:19 back to Port Washington. There was no need to stay any longer. With Dolores in New York, everything was under control.

"What about the other relatives? Isn't there anyone else who should know?"

Her father reached for a packet of mustard. Tearing it open, he squeezed a thick yellow ribbon onto his burger.

"No one." Mar's mother shook her head. "Pearl brought it down on herself. It's her own fault."

Silencing his wife with a glance, her father said, "It's no one's fault. Life was hard for Chinese women."

"What do you mean, Dad?"

"I mean life was hard."

Still not understanding, Mar looked at him, waiting for the rest of the answer.

"When life's hard, the world comes down to Us and Them. If you're not a friend, you're an enemy."

A few minutes later, they stood outside the hospital. While her father hailed a cab, Mar and her mother embraced good-bye. Forehead crinkling with worry, her mother said, "You'll take a cab, too? It's late."

"Of course I will."

After watching her mother's face recede into the sea of red taillights, she walked down Second Avenue to St. Mark's Church. Chrysanthemums glowed coldly behind the iron bars. In the churchyard huddled a dozen or so people, some of them smoking, the aftermath of a poetry reading. Seated on the stone base of the fence was the homeless woman Mar gave money to. With her many-layered skirts stretched between her legs, she was a mad version of a country woman on her porch. Instead of begging in the cold city night, she might just have well have been shelling peas.

Groping in her bag for some change, Mar found only the fortune she'd gotten at the Buddhist temple.

"Sorry, I'm all out."

The woman stared at her blankly, as if she'd never seen her before.

Back in her apartment, Mar sat cross-legged on the floor before the portraits of Pearl and her great-grandfather. Although the Qing Dynasty painting and 1940s studio portrait couldn't have been more different in style, they both served to disguise their subjects instead of revealing them. Pearl and the great-grandfather, whose name she'd never learned, were so tightly wrapped in the winding sheets of their times that they were impossible to see. The starlet and the warlord. They seemed separated not by a generation, but by centuries. *Us and Them.* How little they must have understood each other.

Reaching into her bag, she took out the fortune, then worked the rubber band off the scroll. She had drawn Fortune Number 35.

Probability of Success: Good.
Enhanced shall be the Splendors of a Flower.

More Stories shall be added to a High Tower.
Wines shall be well kept least they become Sour.
Machines shall always be producing Power.

So this was the fortune she'd been so unwilling to accept as her own. The series of statements in awkward, flowery English was supposed to add up to her destiny, but she had no real idea what they meant. The words built a weird, garish structure that she circled, not knowing whether it was a castle, hospital, prison, or tomb.

She had believed Pearl to be a brave outlaw who defied the constraints of two cultures for the sake of love. *Life was hard for Chinese women.* All along she'd just been struggling to survive. Maybe she had never really known Pearl, who, for her survival, paid the awful price of being alone.

The following day after work, Mar returned to Bellevue with the portraits of Pearl and her great-grandfather in her backpack. The man on the ventilator was gone. There instead was a skeletal old woman with white puffs of hair. A tube held in place by green-tinged tape disappeared down her nose.

Mar's shoulders tightened with tension. Walking slowly, she stopped behind the blue curtain that half enclosed Pearl's bed.

Nothing seemed to have changed. Pearl sat upright against the pillows, the hand with the IV tube gripping the TV remote. Her glassy eyes, the wounded one still bright with hemorrhaged blood, were trained toward the ceiling. Dolores was seated on the radiator cover. In her hands was a paperback novel. On the cover, embracing, were a white woman and man dressed in antebellum-era clothing. An unreadable title looped above their heads in gold script.

Dolores glanced up from her book. Mar's breath caught, but Dolores, unseeing, turned the page.

For the next hour and a half, Mar waited in the solarium across from the bank of elevators. A man her father's age, in wool slacks and a white shirt with the sleeves rolled up, slept on one of the couches, his eyelids trembling with dreams. When visiting hours were almost over, Mar saw Dolores's black-and-white form pass the doorway. Just to be safe, she waited five minutes more before emerging into the empty hall.

After she stepped behind the blue curtain, Pearl looked up at her, then back at the TV.

"I can't get this thing to work," she said. "You give it a try."

Settling onto the foot of Pearl's bed, Mar took the remote. Pearl's hair, flattened against the back of her head, looked greasy. When Mar told Matthew about her last visit, he said that hospitalization could unmask, in an older person, dementia that might otherwise have gone unnoticed. When Mar shook her head no, he gently added that head trauma could cause a patient's personality to change overnight. "What do you mean?" said Mar, who thought people were essentially immune to change. What was mistaken for change was really a kind of unfolding, the way roses unfolded, the shape of each new petal dictated by the last.

On the screen was a pair of women's hands, splayed as if in astonishment. Between them dangled a chain on which hung the outline of a heart studded with diamonds, or what passed for diamonds.

"What do you want to see?" Mar asked.

"I don't care. They keep it on all day to torture me."

"Should I turn it off?"

Pearl's eyes widened with panic. "No, that's not allowed."

Mar switched channels until the screen filled with the murky green water of some nameless sea. The lens of the camera lifted above the surface, into the light and splashing waves.

"How's this?"

"Turn it up," Pearl said. "I want to hear the words." Apparently satisfied, she nodded. "They never leave me in peace. How can anyone get any sleep?"

The scene now was from above, as if shot from a helicopter flying low over the water. A whale's cloven tail broke the surface, then splashed thunderously down.

"Do you know who I am?"

Pearl looked at her warily. "I don't have any blood left. You took it all."

"I didn't take your blood."

"What do you want now?"

What *did* she want? Was it love that drew her, or obligation? What did she want from anyone, except help in staving off the loneliness that surrounded her like the darkness just beyond the streetlights' glow.

"To see you. I came here to see you." Mar drew the photograph and the portrait from her backpack and laid them on Pearl's knees.

Pearl ran a finger over the frame that contained the image of her younger self.

"What's this?"

"A gift."

"It's too heavy. Take it away."

Although she didn't move, Pearl seemed to shrink in size. She *had* changed after all. She had grown gentle and vague. The fight was gone out of her, or maybe she'd finally given up. The woman in the photo had become a stranger. Mar was already a stranger. And she realized, too late, that for all their time together she had never taken a picture of Pearl. Whatever images she might want to create would have to be drawn from memory.

"They say my heart needs help. After they put the machine in here"—Pearl gestured at her chest—"Dolores is taking me to Florida."

When Mar didn't answer, Pearl closed her eyes. "I wish I'd been born a bird in a golden cage, so I could sing all day and never have to die."

The voice on the television, a man's voice, said the humpback whales' breeding grounds were being compromised. This, the voice said, might prove to be the coup de grâce.

Tears stood in Mar's eyes. Nodding sagely, Pearl said, "Everyone's got their problems."

Two months later, Mar found herself walking with Matthew down to Chinatown. On Mulberry Street, green garlands hung between the streetlights. At the zenith of every arch was a white rabbit holding a decorated egg between its paws.

"I see Easter came early this year."

Mar laced her arm through his. "It's for New Year's, the Year of the Rabbit."

"But this is Little Italy."

"They're showing some solidarity. Anything wrong with that?"

They crossed Canal. Red-and-gold banners hung in

the windows. The fruit-stand stalls were piled high with oranges. Stirred by memories, Mar told Matthew about the New Years of her childhood: the firecrackers, the undulating lion, the people who would greet her grandfather, then give her red envelopes with clean new one- or five-dollar bills inside.

"The world was bigger then, scarier and more inviting."

"That's great," Matthew said. "All I remember about New Year's is going to parties where they served pigs-in-a-blanket and onion dip, and while the grown-ups got drunk, we watched Dick Clark."

"Now that we're the grown-ups, New Year's means you clean your house and pay your debts."

"So have you?"

She laughed. "You've seen my house. You don't want to know about my debts."

They were standing in front of the temple on Bowery, the same temple where she'd first seen Pearl. The fluorescent light that illuminated the storefront window was turned on, washing the Buddhas and bodhisattvas in its bluish glow. Mar gazed at the Goddess of Mercy, the polished teak of her flowing gown as smooth as water. For a moment, the sadness she felt didn't have a source.

"This one's Kuan Yin," she said. The memory of the woman praying in front of the window took shape. Now she remembered the women seated inside—Pearl among them—who had watched her select the bound scrap of words.

"Even I know that," Matthew said. "What's the stuff pouring out of her vase?"

"Mercy, I guess."

"Every religion has its merciful woman."

The sadness stayed with her through dim sum and the

walk back uptown. Neither she nor her parents had heard from Dolores. Even the yearly Christmas card hadn't come. She imagined they wouldn't hear until Pearl died, if then. *A boneyard full of sun.* Pearl was already in a kind of purgatory. Next came nothingness—the Buddhist nothingness or the other nothingness Mar suspected lay ahead for them all.

She imagined trying to explain her feelings to Matthew. *I'm sad about Pearl.* How ordinary the words would sound. How little they would convey her complicated sense of loss.

They reached her apartment. The awkward days of not knowing whether he'd want to come up again after a night together were over. She and Matthew were in the comfortable stage of love. *Enhanced shall be the Splendors of a Flower.* No, it didn't fit. *More Stories shall be added to a High Tower.* That didn't fit, either. One day she might leave him or he her, but for now they were together.

He waited while she turned the key in the mailbox, which contained an American Express bill and two offers for pre-approved credit cards. The last piece was a small manila envelope addressed in a childish block print. No return address. The cancellation mark, red lines emanating from a pale red sun, said Tampa.

Filled with foreboding, she tore the envelope open. Inside was a bundle of keys held together by a thin pink rubber band someone had twisted again and again over the metal teeth. With a start, she recognized the keys as her own.

She squeezed the torn mouth of the envelope open, but of course there was no note.

"What is it?" Matthew asked.

A vital force had touched her, then passed out of her

life. All along the prophecy had been Pearl. Perhaps the day's sadness grew from the foreknowledge that she'd find what Pearl had returned. Her great-aunt hadn't neglected to clean her own house, stripping Mar from her life forever.

"Remember Pearl?"

"How could I forget?"

Mar tried to unwrap the bundle, but the rubber band was too tightly wound. Finally, she slipped the keys into her bag and, with Matthew following behind, began the long climb back to her uncleaned home.

JOCELYN LIEU's fiction has appeared in anthologies and literary journals, including *Charlie Chan Is Dead: An Anthology of Contemporary American Fiction*, *110 Stories: New York Writes after September 11*, the *Denver Quarterly*, and the *Asian Pacific American Journal*. A graduate of the MFA Program for Writers at Warren Wilson College, she currently teaches writing at Parsons School of Design/ New School University.

The text of this book has been set in Berling,
a typeface designed by the Swedish typographer
and calligrapher Karl-Erik Forsberg.

Book design by Wendy Holdman.
Typesetting by Stanton Publication Services, Inc.
Manufactured by Friesens on acid-free paper.